THE
CINCO DE MAYO
MURDER

**Center Point
Large Print**

THE
CINCO DE MAYO
MURDER

LEE HARRIS

CENTER POINT PUBLISHING
THORNDIKE, MAINE

This book is dedicated to
Joe Blades
for at least twenty reasons.

This Center Point Large Print edition
is published in the year 2007 by arrangement with
The Random House Publishing Group,
a division of Random House, Inc.

The text of this Large Print edition is unabridged. In other
aspects, this book may vary from the original edition. Printed in
Thailand. Set in 16-point Times New Roman type.

ISBN: 1-58547-909-8
ISBN 13: 978-1-58547-909-2

Library of Congress Cataloging-in-Publication Data

Harris, Lee, 1935-
    The Cinco de Mayo murder / Lee Harris.--Center Point large print ed.
       p. cm.
    ISBN-13: 978-1-58547-909-2 (lib. bdg. : alk. paper)
    1. Bennett, Christine (Fictitious character)--Fiction. 2. Cinco de Mayo (Mexican
holiday)--Fiction. 3. Large type books. 4. Arizona--Fiction. I. Title.

PS3562.E23C56 2007
813'.54--dc22

2006026715

ACKNOWLEDGMENTS

I thank James L. V. Wegman for his help in this and all my mysteries. Without him, I could not have achieved such a high level of accuracy and realism; and Carol Hovasse for her help in showing me parts of Tucson that I didn't know existed.

I also wish to thank all the wonderful women who have made my love for Arizona even greater than the feelings evoked by the natural beauty of the state: Carol Hovasse, Jane Candia Coleman, Carol Walsh, Laurie Colen, Joan McGarry, Barb Bartley, Carolyn Emery, Bobbe Idaspe, Barb Witwer, Regina Wegman, Pam Helmandollar, Bennie McGarry, Marilyn Merryweather, and Carol Zehren.

And a special thank you to Blake Koolick, my #1 fan.

What is the price of a thousand horses against a son where there is one son only?

—"Riders to the Sea,"
JOHN MILLINGTON SYNGE

He whom the gods favor dies in youth.

—"Bacchides,"
PLAUTUS

1

In the years since I was released from my vows at St. Stephen's Convent, I have learned to expect almost anything when the phone rings. I have received the usual good news and bad news that is part of everyone's life, and in addition I have heard extraordinary and frightening messages. Last year someone called to say that a murder would take place, after which I heard a gunshot.

So if I answer the phone reluctantly or with hesitation, it's not hard to understand why. But on a rainy day in April, I was thinking of other things as I walked toward the ring, picked up the phone, and said, "Hello."

"Chris, it's Joseph. I hope everyone is well."

Sister Joseph is the General Superior of the convent where I spent fifteen years of my life, many of them as a Franciscan nun. Above and beyond that, she is my closest friend, and hearing her voice always makes me happy.

"Joseph, what a pleasure to hear from you. We're fine, looking forward to some dry weather before we all sink into the mud."

"We have the same problem here. If you take a step off the walkway, it's at your peril. But I have something warmer and drier to talk about."

"I'm listening."

"There's a conference next month in Phoenix, Arizona, that I've been asked to attend. Besides the fact that I've never been out there, the topic of discussion is important to St. Stephen's. We're going to discuss the problem of too few novices and too many aging nuns in American convents."

"Not a topic I enjoy thinking about."

"True, but one I'm forced to think about more and more. I'll be flying out to Phoenix the first Saturday of May. The conference will begin on Monday and last until mid-week. Then I'd like to take a day or two to visit Tucson. There's a beautiful old mission there that I've always wanted to visit."

"It sounds like a wonderful trip, Joseph," I said, thinking that she deserved it.

"I'm really looking forward to it, especially the Tucson part. I've received permission to rent a car for part of my stay, so getting to Tucson won't be a problem. What I'm calling about is whether you might be interested in accompanying me."

There was a silence and I realized I was supposed to respond, but I was so startled I didn't know what to say. "Travel with you?" I finally managed to get out.

"I would enjoy having a traveling companion, and there's no one I'd rather share the trip with than you."

"Joseph . . . that's a wonderful invitation. I would love to do it. But I can't give you an answer right now. I'm sure you understand."

"Of course I understand. There's Eddie to think of, and Jack's needs, too. I just wanted to tell you about it and see if you think it might work out. The diocese will pay for the hotel rooms, which should make it more reasonable. Also the car. I'm so glad you're enthusiastic. Think it over and give me a call when you've discussed it with your family."

"We'll talk about it tonight. Thank you so much."

"And I won't drag you to dull meetings. You'll be on your own. I assume that's something that will please you."

"You bet."

"I look forward to hearing from you, then."

I hung up and sat down. All I could think was, Wow! Arizona, the Southwest, Phoenix, Tucson, an old mission. What a fantastic piece of luck, and how fortunate I would be to do it with a person who was as anxious as I to see everything, to leave nothing undone. I began to look at my calendar, to try to figure out how I could have Eddie taken care of without impinging on Jack's work schedule. He was now a lieutenant at NYPD and often had to work weekends. That was a lot better than the nights he'd worked when he was first appointed, but it did limit our family time.

I went upstairs to the closet where we kept our collection of maps. In an atlas of the country I found the page for Arizona. Besides Phoenix and Tucson, the Grand Canyon was there, a place that I had often dreamed of visiting, but Joseph's schedule sounded too tight.

After Eddie came home from school, I waited another half hour and called Mel, my neighbor across the street. She has been teaching in what we in Oakwood call the little school—K through four—for a couple of years,

9

and often gets home after the children.

"Chris, hi, how are you? I've been so busy with our class project, I've neglected my friends."

"I'm fine. We're all fine. Is this a bad time to talk?"

"Not at all. Why don't you drag Eddie over? Noah's here, Sari's somewhere else. I'll have to look at my calendar to find out where."

I laughed. "Sounds like you need a personal secretary."

"I do. It's just I can't pay anyone. Oh, here it is, Brownies. Someone's taking her home so I'm off the hook. Come over."

"On my way."

Mel was the first person I'd met after moving into Aunt Meg's house when I was released from my vows. Something clicked between us and we became friends. At the time she had two young children, while I was still single and feeling my way around a secular world that in some ways I hardly knew. Happily for both of us, when Jack and I married, our husbands took to each other and became friends as well. Mel helped me navigate my way into life in Oakwood, not an easy job for someone who had been cloistered her entire adult life.

Eddie was happy, as always, to visit Mel and any children who might be around. Besides the attraction of friends, he knew there were always delicious cookies in the Gross house; he never had to be asked twice. He ran down the street ahead of me and waited impatiently at the door as I took my time on the walk, admiring the shrubs and spring flowers.

"Come in, come in," Mel called, seeing Eddie on her

doorstep. "Chris, I tried that jasmine rice at Prince's and it's great. Goes with that chicken stir-fry I told you about."

"I tried the stir-fry. You were right. It was easy and quick and Jack loved it. Maybe I'll give the jasmine rice a try, too."

"So what's new? Doing any work for Arnold?"

Arnold Gold is my lawyer friend from New York. He farms out word processing jobs to me when I'm available and his staff—which isn't very large—is overworked. "I'm just finishing something, and I have to go over it carefully," I replied. "There's a lot of language that's more legal than I'm used to, and the sentences don't always make sense to me." I turned to Eddie. "Eddie, what are you doing?"

"Just looking at the magazine."

"You can read it if you want," Mel said. "Noah's upstairs if you'd like to visit with him. He has some new software."

"Games?"

"I'm pretty sure he has games." Mel turned to me. "Isn't that what computers are all about? We keep trying to get the kids to learn interesting things and all they want to do is play games."

"They're learning," I assured her. "What a world."

"Eddie, take some cookies upstairs. Here, I'll get you a couple of napkins."

She received one of Eddie's best smiles for her trouble. As he mounted the stairs, carefully holding cookies and napkins, I heard the teakettle begin to whistle. We would sip tea as we talked.

As we sat a few minutes later, I told Mel about the phone call from Joseph.

"That's wonderful, Chris. You'll just love the South-west. We did. Hal thought we might consider buying a second home out there someday, if we can ever afford to send these kids to college and still have anything left. Where will you go?"

I told her what I knew of Joseph's wishes and itin-erary. "We won't get to the Grand Canyon but I can visit places around Phoenix while she's in her meetings. Then we'll drive down to Tucson—it doesn't look very far on the map—and see an old mission she's wanted to visit for years."

"Probably San Xavier. It's quite beautiful. You see it off to the right as you drive south on I-19. It's perfectly white and domed. The sanctuary is beautiful, and there's a museum in the building. You can go to mass there on Sunday morning, too."

"I don't know if we'll be there that long. Listen to me, I haven't even talked to Jack about it yet."

"He won't mind," Mel said as though Jack were her brother. "He's a good sport."

That was true. "What's the food like?" I asked. I'm not what Jack calls an adventurous eater, although I have improved with age.

"Yummy. There's lots of Mexican. If you like gua-camole and refried beans and enchiladas—"

"I don't even know what you're talking about. Well, I hope it works out."

"Of course it'll work out," my optimistic friend declared. "I'll talk to Hal tonight and make a list of the places we loved so you'll have an edge when you get there. When did you say you were going?"

"May."

"It'll be hot in May, but who cares? Everything's air-conditioned and whatever hotel you stay in will have a pool."

"It sounds wonderful," I said.

"It is. You'll see."

We talked for about an hour, Mel discussing some classes she thought she'd like to take. She's a very enterprising and dedicated teacher and has wanted for some time to get a master's degree. When I finally dragged Eddie downstairs, Mel put some cookies in a plastic bag, allegedly for Jack, but I knew I would have to rescue them or none would be left when Jack got home.

Eddie had some homework to do, reading and answering questions, so he sat at the kitchen table as I put dinner together. Soon Jack came home, on time for a change. He was an "administrative lieutenant in charge of planning/coordination of special projects" in the Midtown South Precinct, MTS—which could mean a demonstration to stop the war, a major rock concert, or anything in between. Although the precinct covers only .77 square mile, it includes Grand Central Station, the jewelry district, the Empire State Building, and numerous other famous locations where trouble can erupt. MTS is called the busiest station house in the world, and I have become a master at keeping food warm while waiting for Jack's return.

"So how's my family?" he said as he hugged first me and then Eddie.

"I'm doing my homework," Eddie said. "We went to Mel's house and she gave me cookies."

"She gave *us* cookies, young man," I corrected.

"I'll bet she said they were for *me,*" Jack said.

I smiled. "She did, actually. And we've even managed to save you a few."

"*I* saved them for you," Eddie declared. "Because I know you like them."

"Good man. So what's new?" He went to the refrigerator and poured himself some juice, then opened the cookie drawer and took a handful of pretzels.

"There is something new," I said, setting melon on the table and turning the fire off under our dinner.

"Don't tell me." Jack gave me a look.

"Nothing like that," I said, knowing he suspected I'd gotten hooked into solving a murder once again. They seem to fall in my lap, no matter where I am.

"Whew."

I poured Eddie's milk and sat at my place. Then I told him about Joseph's invitation.

"Do it," he said without giving it any critical thought. "I bet Mom would love to come out and take over while you're gone."

"I was kind of thinking that."

"I'll give her a call tonight. Think you'd like Grandma out here for a few days, Eddie?"

14

"Where's Mommy going?"

I explained. He knows all the nuns at St. Stephen's; we've visited there often since he was born.

"That's OK. Grandma cooks good food, too."

I wasn't sure whether he was referring to me, to Jack, or to Mel, and I didn't ask. "And I bet she'd have fun helping you with your homework."

"I don't need help. But she could read to me at night."

It sounded as though my trip was practically a sure thing. After Eddie was in bed, Jack called his parents. His mother was jubilant. It didn't matter what the dates were: she would arrange to be free. I took the phone and we talked for a while. You would have thought I was doing her a special favor instead of the reverse.

After the call, we talked about the trip over coffee and rescued cookies. Jack slipped a couple over to me almost surreptitiously, as though Eddie might be sneaking a peek.

Then we returned to our respective reading with occasional comments to each other. The phone rang and Jack got up and answered. I listened, hoping nothing was happening at the station house that required his driving back in to Manhattan. Happily, it was just a follow-up report, and he rejoined me in the family room, telling me who had called. I had become familiar with many of the precinct names over the last year and felt as though I knew some of them personally, although I had met very few of the cops in his command.

After he resumed his reading, something fluttered to

the surface of my mind. Arizona. Mountains. Someone I once knew.

"You look as if you're far away," Jack said as I peered into the distance.

"I am. Twenty years or so back. Someone I once knew went to Arizona. It was a boy I went to high school with before I went to St. Stephen's to live."

"What's the significance?"

"I don't know yet. I can't even remember his name."

"Is this ominous? Should I check my weapon?"

I gave him a grin. "Not yet. I think I'll go upstairs and find my high school yearbooks. Maybe it'll light a fire in my memory."

As it happened, it didn't. I turned pages, looked at pictures, read names that I hadn't thought of for a couple of decades. I was closer to forty now than thirty and although many of the names and photos were familiar, only one really meant anything to me—that of my friend Madeleine. We had spoken about six months before but hadn't managed to get together. I had been best friends with her before I left high school for St. Stephen's. Not long before I was married, Maddie had invited me to the baptism of her first child. It took place in a wonderful old church in central New York State in Studsburg, a town that didn't exist anymore. Thirty years earlier, the small village had been emptied and the Army Corps of Engineers had made a lake out of the area, which had the natural shape of a basin. The purpose was to avoid floods in the farm region around Studsburg. At the time that Maddie called, a persistent drought had dried up the lake and revealed the foundations of houses as well as the perfectly preserved Catholic church, where the christening took place after a thorough cleaning.

I reached for the phone on my office desk and dialed Maddie's number. She was elated to hear my voice, and we spent several minutes catching up on family news. Finally I told her about my impending trip to Arizona.

"Maddie," I said, "something happened in Arizona a long time ago. It had to do with a boy in our high school class, but I can't remember the name. Am I ringing any bells?"

"Absolutely. It was Heinz Gruner."

"Yes! Of course. I remember now. Hold on a second." I leafed through the open yearbook and found a picture of him, a somber, round-faced boy who looked as though he had not yet learned to smile. "Here he is. What a sad kid he was."

"That's the one. He was a nice enough guy, but he was so introverted. I don't think he had many friends."

"What's the story? What's the connection to Arizona?"

"It was very sad, Chris. He traveled out there one summer when he was in college to walk in the mountains, and he disappeared. Some hikers found his body several days later. It looked as if he had fallen off a narrow trail. He probably died in the fall or soon after."

"I remember now. It was in the paper. Aunt Meg sent me the clipping. There wasn't any evidence of foul play, was there?"

17

"Not at all. The question they raised was whether he had slipped and fallen or whether—" She stopped, and I knew what she was thinking.

"Whether he committed suicide?"

"Yes. It's terrible to think of a kid of nineteen or twenty doing something like that. Traveling all that way by himself, finding a lonely trail. Even now it's hard for me to say it."

"Why would he do that?" I asked.

"You remember him, Chris. Smart, quiet, almost no friends. I don't think he ever went out on a date or got invited to a party. He spent all his time in the library or at home with his parents. His father was very stiff. I met him once, maybe at high school graduation. Mrs. Gruner was there, too, kind of a mousy woman. Maybe I'm being unfair, but I swear she walked two steps behind him."

"I remember her," I said. "We met a couple of times, at school functions, I think. She was very sweet."

"Yes, she used to help out at concerts and plays."

I hadn't graduated from Maddie's high school, having gone to live at St. Stephen's when I was about halfway through. From then on, I attended high school in the town adjacent to the convent. "Where did he go to college?" I asked.

"I don't remember, some small, elite place in Ohio or Indiana or one of those states. I never saw him after graduation. No, that's wrong—I did, just once. I was out on a date, I think, and we stopped at Blackie's Diner for ice cream after a movie. Doesn't that sound

18

sweet and innocent?" She laughed.

Never having dated in my life till I was released from my vows at age thirty, I was hardly the judge of sweetness and innocence. But I agreed with her that it did. "And you saw him?"

"He was in a booth with a girl I'd never seen and they were eating huge sundaes. Funny that I remember that. When my date and I left the diner, we walked past the table and I said hi. It took him a couple of seconds to place me, but I got a smile from him. That was the last time I saw him. He probably died the next summer."

I felt a chill. We were talking about a real person whom we had known, someone who had figured in our lives. "I don't suppose you remember where in Arizona he died."

"Oh gosh no. It wasn't the Grand Canyon. I'd remember that. It was a mountain somewhere. Tucson sticks in my mind."

"Mine, too. Are his parents alive?"

"I'm not sure. I think I read an obituary for his father a long time ago. They weren't young. I think Heinz was born when his parents were already close to middle age. They came over from Germany or Austria after the war and they spoke with an accent, but their English was excellent. I think Heinz was born here."

"So his mother might be alive," I said.

"Could be. Hold on, I'll check the phone book." She put the phone down and I sat and waited. Maddie still lived in the town where we'd grown up, several miles from the house where I'd been raised. Her mention of

Blackie's Diner had triggered a host of memories, all pleasant. I could almost taste the hot fudge they were famous for, which we ate by the gallon.

"There's no Gruner in the book," Maddie's voice said in my ear. "And this is for several towns around. So either Mrs. Gruner moved or died or—"

"Or remarried," I said.

"Why are you so interested, Chris?"

I told her about my upcoming trip to Arizona and how it had brought back memories. "In any case, I think I'll try to locate Mrs. Gruner and have a chat with her before I go. I haven't thought of Heinz since the time I read about his death. I'm sure she'd like to hear from someone who thought her son was a nice person."

"Sounds like you're describing a mother."

"I am indeed. Let's get together, Maddie, when you and I have a free day or at least a couple of hours."

"After Easter," she said. "Things should calm down. Give my love to Jack."

"I will." I asked to be remembered to her family as well, including her parents. Then I hung up and thought about the boy who died so far from home so many years too soon.

2

I didn't mention my interest in Heinz Gruner to Jack. Since I was unlikely to find his mother and even more unlikely to learn anything further about his untimely death, it didn't merit a discussion. Besides Maddie, I

20

knew almost no one else from high school. My short time there had not been happy. My mother was ill and she died when I was fifteen, my father having died of a heart attack a number of years earlier. I'd gone to live with Aunt Meg and Uncle Willy but their home was also a place of illness, notably my cousin Gene's. That I emerged as a whole person was due to the efforts of the nuns at St. Stephen's, with the help of my aunt and uncle. Despite all the trouble in their lives, they remained a constant support.

I called Joseph the next morning to tell her that I was happy to accept her invitation, and that all the arrangements for my family would be taken care of. She said she would let me know soon what her dates were, what hotel we would stay at in Phoenix, and other details. I checked my wardrobe and found that last year's bathing suits were still in good shape and my summer clothes were just waiting to be packed.

While I was reading the *Times* after lunch, the phone rang. It was Maddie.

"I made a couple of phone calls this morning," she said. "Believe it or not, I located Mrs. Gruner."

"Maddie, that's wonderful. I think I'll enlist you if I ever have another homicide to solve. Where is she?"

"In a care facility. There's a home not far from here: one of those places that's split between older people who need almost no care and go about their business, and people who need assistance. Mrs. Gruner had a stroke several years ago and she's been there ever since. Here's the number of the home."

I grabbed an envelope and wrote it down. "Maybe I'll drive over this afternoon. Eddie is taken care of after school, and my teaching work is done."

"You're too much," Maddie said, laughing. "You think you're going to find a murder in that poor boy's death?"

"Not at all. I think I'm going to keep a lonesome mother company for an hour and listen to whatever she wants to talk about."

"Keep me informed."

I promised to do that.

I called the home and was told Mrs. Gruner was able to have visitors and this afternoon would be a fine time to come. I didn't need an explicit invitation. I took off.

Hillside Village sat on a large, beautiful piece of property that would be green in a few weeks. It wasn't exactly a "village," but several buildings formed the complex, most of them small, one-story affairs. That was where the independent residents lived, I learned later. The large central structure housed those people who needed assistance or nursing care. Lawn furniture dotted the area in front of that building, but it was too cool for sitting outside. I parked in the visitors' section around the side and found my way inside to the front desk where it was warm, and people walked or were pushed in wheelchairs along the hallway.

"I'm Chris Bennett," I announced to the young woman at the desk. "I called awhile ago. I'd like to visit Mrs. Gruner."

"Yes, I took your call. I'll tell her you're coming."
She tried the number, but no one answered. "She may be sleeping or at an activity. Let me get someone to show you the way."

It took several minutes before a young man appeared wearing a name tag that said ERNIE, and he accompanied me to an elevator and up to the third floor.

"You a relative?" he asked.

"I'm Christine Bennett, an old friend of her son."

"Her son. Yeah. She talks about him. He died, didn't he?"

"Many years ago. We went to the same high school."

"I bet she'll be glad to see you. She doesn't get many visitors."

The elevator stopped and we marched down the corridor. Ernie was a fast walker and although I walk pretty fast myself, I had to hurry to keep up. He stopped abruptly in front of a closed door. I had noticed as we scampered down the hall that most of the doors were open.

He knocked and called, "Mrs. Gruner, you have a visitor. Can we come in?" When a sound reached us, he opened the door. "Hi, Mrs. Gruner. This is Christine Bennett. She's come to see you."

The woman sitting in the chair by the window observed us with sharp eyes. "I know you," she said, her English heavily accented. "The face is familiar but I don't remember the name."

"Chris Bennett. I went to high school with Heinz."

"Yes, of course. You knew my son."

"Well," Ernie said, "I'll leave you two together." He closed the door behind him.

I sat on the bottom edge of the bed, which was covered with a spread. "We met a few times when we both helped out at school events," I said. "And I knew Heinz. I went to his high school for about two years."

"Yes, I remember now. We talked while we set the tables. What brings you here after all this time?"

"I thought about Heinz yesterday and I asked an old friend where his parents were. I just thought I'd like to drop in and say hello." As I spoke, I had the sense that perhaps I shouldn't have come. It had been impulsive of me to drive here without first asking Mrs. Gruner if she wanted company. Her life of solitude might be a personal choice.

"You thought about Heinz? What did you think?"

"His name came up in conversation," I said. "I remember him very well. Is there anything I can get you, Mrs. Gruner? Some tea?"

"Tea. Yes, I like a cup of tea. You will get it?"

"I'll be right back." I looked around, hoping to find a nurse or an aide who could help me. I retraced my steps to the elevator, continued beyond it, and found a nurse's station. I explained my mission, and one of the nurses said she would have two cups of tea sent to Mrs. Gruner's room. I thanked her and found my way back. "They'll send up some tea."

The woman smiled and nodded. I wondered if she ever asked for anything or if she just sat and accepted

24

what was given to her. She had a plain face, marked with lines that did not come from laughter. Her hair was straight and coarse, fading black mixed with colorless gray. She wore no makeup. Her skin was sallow. She was wearing a black wool skirt and a gray cotton blouse with a black sweater over it.

"I like tea," she said again. "Do you like tea?"

"Very much. Especially on a gray afternoon."

"I have not gone out." She turned and looked out the window. "Yes, it is gray." She turned back to look at me. "Tell me your name again?"

"Chris Bennett. I went to school with Heinz for a couple of years. Then I left the area."

"You know my son is dead."

"Yes, I heard about it. My aunt sent me the article from the paper. I should have written you a letter. I'm sorry I didn't."

"He's buried next to my husband. I have not been to the cemetery for many years."

"Are you able to walk?"

She pointed to a cane with three prongs on the bottom. "I need a little help, but I can walk. I used to walk every morning before my stroke. How did you know Heinz?"

"We were in a couple of classes together. I liked him very much."

"He was a good son, a good person. When he died, he killed both of us."

"It must have been terrible."

"Terrible? Terrible is a war or an avalanche or an epidemic. When your son dies, it is the end of the world."

"Yes," I said, humbled by her description. "You're right."

"He was our only child, the one who would carry something of us forward into future generations as he made himself a life. I'm sorry. I should talk of other things. We are not friends, only acquaintances. The German language makes a difference between friends and acquaintances. Did you know that?"

"I don't know German. But it sounds like a useful distinction."

"That is what it is. I had friends, good friends, in Germany. One or two of them have come to visit. My husband and I went to visit several times, but I cannot travel alone. So those friends are gone. We had friends here, too, but most have left for other places. Some have died. I sound like a dreary old woman."

"You sound as though you've thought a lot about life and its consequences."

"Consequences, yes."

As she started to elaborate, there was a knock on the door and a girl came in with a tray. She set it on top of the dresser, asked if there was anything else she could do, and left.

The tea was in a ceramic pot with two cups and saucers and a dish of cookies on a white paper doily. I poured for both of us. Mrs. Gruner took lemon, as I did, and declined sugar. She took two cookies and set them on her lap. The tea was hot and aromatic. I was glad I'd ordered it.

26

"We gave him the money to take the trip," she said, continuing her last thought. "He enjoyed hiking. At college he had friends who spent the weekends walking and hiking. It was our birthday present to him, the ticket to Arizona so he could see the desert and all the mountains out there. They said he fell from the trail. He had many injuries."

"That's what I heard."

She nibbled at a cookie. "My husband went out to see the place," she said. "He walked the same trail where Heinz walked. He said Heinz was too sure—" She stopped, searching for a word.

"Sure-footed," I supplied.

"Yes, sure on his feet. He should not have fallen."

"Accidents happen, Mrs. Gruner. Maybe the sun was hot and he felt light-headed. He could have run out of water and not felt steady on his feet."

"This is all possible." She set her cup and saucer down on a small table beside her.

I brought the pot over and refilled the cup, then warmed up my own.

"Thank you," she said. "I enjoy a cup of tea in the afternoon but I forget to ask for it. And you know what I do when I'm finished?" Her eyes lit up. "I eat the lemon." She smiled. "My husband could never understand it. He needed sugar in everything. I like the tart taste of lemons and limes and grapefruits."

"So do I," I admitted. "Maybe we come from the same family."

She nodded and smiled. "It's good to talk to someone

who isn't complaining about the food or her daughter-in-law."

I laughed. "Not very stimulating conversation."

"But better than thinking over and over about what happened twenty years ago. If we could only go back and do it again."

"Are you able to go out for a drive?" I asked, trying to divert her to a different topic of conversation.

"I cannot drive."

"But you could sit next to me."

"I can sit next to anyone."

"Suppose I come back and we'll go out for a ride."

"Why do you do this?" she asked. "We are only acquaintances."

"Because I want to," I said. "Would you like to go?"

"Very much. Very, very much."

"I'll call and arrange a date. It's been a pleasure meeting you, Mrs. Gruner."

"Thank you, Mrs. Bennett."

"Chris. Call me Chris."

She pronounced my name. Her R's were very German but she spoke English well. She held out her hand for me to shake. Then I left.

Jack listened to my story that evening. "How did you find her?" he asked.

"Maddie found her. She doesn't get many visitors. She probably sits inside in the winter and outside in the summer and goes nowhere. That's no way to live. I'm going to take her for a ride next week, let her look around and breathe some fresh air."

"From what you said, it sounds like she thinks her son committed suicide."

"She didn't say that. She just said it was unlikely that someone with his hiking skills would fall. I told her it was very possible that he did. He could have been dehydrated; it gets pretty hot down there. Or maybe the sun made him disoriented. People shouldn't hike alone in unknown territory."

"Agreed. So don't you do that when you're there." He gave me a look.

"I'll be as good as I can. If I wander off on a trail, I'll have Joseph with me."

"Great," he said with sarcasm. "So you're going to try to prove that this guy fell, that he didn't jump off the trail."

"I'm not trying to prove anything. I just want to make a sad old woman happy."

He leaned over and kissed me. "Let's go upstairs and make your ever-lovin' husband happy."

"Sounds good to me."

3

I have been teaching a course at a local college for several years. Most of what we read is mysteries by American women. Occasionally, by popular request, we read a book by a man. I vary the list of books each semester, partly to keep myself from becoming bored and partly to keep my students honest. Looking at last year's final won't help to answer all the questions I ask this year.

I teach one long class every Monday morning, and then I'm free for the rest of the week. I like to have lunch at the college after I teach, as the food is made by students in the food service program and it's unusually good for institutional fare. Also, they sell fresh hot pies, and that will keep me teaching forever if Jack has his way. He's a sucker for fruit pies. Not that Eddie and I aren't.

I checked with Mrs. Gruner on Sunday afternoon to see whether she was up for a drive on Monday. Then I called Elsie Rivers, my mother's closest friend and my ace babysitter. She would pick Eddie up from school and take him to her house until I arrived.

After lunch at the college, I bought a fresh, warm apple pie, and stopped at Prince's, our upscale supermarket, on the way home to get some ice cream. Then I went home to put the food away before driving to Hillside Village. I decided to stay in my teaching clothes, which are somewhat less casual than my at-home clothes. Mrs. Gruner was an Old World woman and would probably appreciate a bit of formality.

She was in the large lobby talking to a woman sitting in a wheelchair when I arrived. Her face lit up as she saw me, and she struggled to her feet as I approached. I had not seen her stand or walk the previous week. Obviously, her stroke had left her with a disability, but she asked for no assistance. She introduced me to the woman next to her and we shook hands. Then Mrs.

Gruner and I walked slowly to the door.

"Where would you like to go?" I asked when we had left Hillside Village behind.

"I would like to go to the cemetery."

"Can you direct me?"

"Yes. But we should buy some flowers first."

"I have them in the backseat," I told her. When I saw her startled face, I added, "I thought you'd like to go. You said it was a long time since you'd been there."

"You are a remarkable woman, Chris."

"Just someone who listens. Tell me where to go."

We were there in twenty minutes. Once inside the gate, we needed directions, which turned out to be easy to follow. Mrs. Gruner held the map in her hand with the route marked in red. Two minutes later I parked the car and helped her out.

The two stones were side by side with room for a third. From the two dates of death, I could see that Heinz's father hadn't lived very long after his son's death—about a year. We divided the flowers between the graves and I stepped back, not wanting to intrude on this profoundly sad experience. I walked among the graves, taking note of the names and the length of the lives, the capsule descriptions: HUSBAND AND FATHER; BELOVED MOTHER; DEAREST CHILD. I glanced back and saw Mrs. Gruner leaning over one of the stones, the cane firmly in one hand, the other on the stone.

A few minutes later when I turned around, she was facing me, and I went back to walk her to the car.

31

"Thank you," she said. "I feel better now. If you still have time—"

"I have lots of time."

"Perhaps we could drive to the sound. I like to look at the water."

The house my family lives in is quite close to the Long Island Sound. In fact, many of the homeowners, including us, own the rights to a cove within walking distance of our house. A sandy beach runs along the edge and the water washes in in gentle waves. It's a place that I love, a place where one can walk in solitude in summer and winter—and of course where one can swim.

I drove Mrs. Gruner there and we got out and walked on the sand. She held my arm and planted the three-pronged cane firmly with every step.

"This is a wonderful place," she said. "I can smell the salt in the air."

"I have a folding chair in the trunk. Would you like to sit?"

"I have been sitting my life away. Today I like to walk."

We walked to the edge where the water lapped at the sand. She seemed transfixed, taking deep breaths as though she could hoard the air for the future.

"My husband was a swimmer," she said. "He would have loved this place. My son was a hiker."

"And you?"

"I was the wife and mother. In Germany I taught school, but here my English was never good enough.

When my husband died, I had nothing."

"You had yourself," I said.

"What was left of me."

A large wave crested and flowed toward the shore. We moved backward as the water covered the spot where we had stood. To my surprise, Mrs. Gruner laughed.

She turned to me, her face happy for the first time since we had met. "How nice that is. When I was a child, we vacationed on the *Nordsee,* the North Sea. We would stand just like this, without our shoes, and feel the water on our feet. A nice memory."

"You had a happy childhood."

"Very happy, all the cousins together, the aunts and uncles. The air was so clean."

"Are you able to get away from Hillside Village very often?"

She looked at me as though I had asked a ridiculous question. "This is my first time in more than a year."

"There are volunteers who—"

"Yes, yes. But I do not like to bother people. I read, I think. The time passes."

We stood on the beach for several minutes as she savored the air and the view. Finally she turned, and we started back to the car. "What I think about is my son."

"Yes."

"You see, it is hard for me to believe that he fell by accident, although what you said about the heat and needing water makes sense to me. The police called it an accident. They said if it wasn't an accident—"

"I understand."

"My son did not kill himself."

"It seems unlikely," I said. I wished I could have said something with more power behind it. A shy person myself, I had not known him well. In the two afternoons I had spent with his mother, we had exchanged more conversation than I ever had with Heinz.

"To us he seemed a happy person. He worked hard in school. He read books. He had a friend that he liked and they talked on the telephone at night."

"Who was that?"

"Donald. I don't remember his last name. He went away to college and never came back. But after Heinz died, I thought about many things. Maybe he seemed too foreign for the children in school. He was born here and he spoke two languages perfectly. But his name was foreign. Maybe we should have called him Harry or Henry instead of giving him such an unusual name as Heinz. In Germany it is not so unusual. Here—" She shrugged. "Maybe the children laughed."

They had laughed. I remembered. They made the obvious jokes about his name. I had heard it happen more than once but although I felt sorry for him, I was too shy to intercede, too shy even to say something nice to him. I pretended I had not heard.

"Children laugh at many things," I said. I looked up at the sky. "Look at the birds."

A flock of seabirds flew over us, turned, and went back over the sound.

"Ah. They are lovely."

34

"Would you like to come to my house and have a cup of tea?"

"Do you live near here?"

"Quite close."

"That would be very nice."

We walked back to the car and I drove the short distance home. The answering machine was beeping annoyingly and I shut it off to keep it quiet. Mrs. Gruner walked with me through the house and into our large family room, the addition we had built after we married.

"What a wonderful fireplace," she said.

"We enjoy a fire at night. It's cozy and warm."

"Yes. You must have a happy life."

"We do. Sit where you're comfortable and I'll make the tea."

We sipped and talked for half an hour. Finally I said, "Mrs. Gruner, I am visiting Arizona in May. I will be quite near the place where Heinz's accident happened." I let her think about it.

"Near the mountain where he hiked?"

"Yes."

"Is it possible—would you have the time—and the interest—to find out about Heinz's accident? If you don't want to—"

"I would like to. My husband is a police officer in New York. He may be able to put me in touch with the right people."

"This is very good of you, Chris."

"I hope I can learn something useful."

I drove her back to Hillside Village. She had some color in her cheeks from the out-of-doors, and she seemed in a good mood. She had asked me to do something important for her and I would do it.

I picked up Eddie and drove home.

"How would you be able to tell the difference between someone falling accidentally and jumping to his death from a trail in the mountains?" I asked Jack when we were together in the family room, a fire burning and coffee in our cups.

"Hard to tell. You want to find proof that this kid you knew didn't kill himself?"

"Mrs. Gruner wants to know what happened. If he did kill himself, I wouldn't tell her. She's been sitting for years thinking about what she did wrong that might have prompted him to take his life. And finding reasons why he didn't."

"Why's she in that home?"

"She had a stroke. She needs a cane to get around, but she's very independent. She doesn't want help if she can do without it. I assume she's not able to live by herself, and I understand her anguish over her son's death."

The phone rang just then and Maddie said, "I found out where Heinz died."

I grabbed a pencil. "I'm listening."

"It's called Picacho Peak. It's somewhere between Tucson and Phoenix. I called the local paper this morning and they researched it for me. I bet you could get a map from the AAA and find it."

"I will do that," I said. I told Maddie I had visited Mrs. Gruner and what we'd talked about.

"They did taunt him," Maddie said. "It was hateful, but it's what teenagers do."

I thanked her for her research and went back to the family room, where Jack had covered my cup with the saucer to keep my coffee warm.

"Sounds like that was Maddie."

"She found out where Heinz died." I showed him the name on the slip of paper.

Jack took it from me. "Tell you what I'll do. I'll find out what town this is and get in touch with the police department or the sheriff's department. See if they can fax me the file. Don't expect this to happen in the next twenty-four hours. With a case this old, they'll have to dig up the file, but they'll have it somewhere."

"You're good," I said.

"Yeah, I'm the best." He gave me the grin that I loved. "I guess I'm glad you save your sympathy for people. I'm not sure I could take it if you picked up stray dogs and cats."

I laughed. "Now, there's an idea."

"Let's just keep it an idea."

It was two weeks before Jack called to say the file had been faxed to him. I had nearly forgotten his promise. He brought it home with him in a thin file folder. Thin meant there weren't any questions. A homicide file is thick and heavy with copies of interviews and all the evidence vouchers, forensics reports, photos, and much

37

more. All that was here were some photographs and the results of the autopsy. The parents had objected to that, but they had been informed it was the law.

Nothing in the autopsy set off any alarms. The ME ruled Heinz's death an accident. He suffered several broken bones, trauma, and concussion. A handwritten letter from the sheriff accompanied the pages. He had no personal knowledge of the accident, as a deputy had been the first on the scene after the call came in that a body had been found. The deputy's first impression was that an unfortunate accident had occurred, and nothing afterward had changed his opinion.

I left the photos for last, not wanting to look at them but feeling I had to. They were black and white. The young man lying in the scrub was the person I remembered. In one of the pictures I could see his glasses lying nearby. I had never seen his face without glasses. I tried to think whether he would have taken them off before jumping if he had taken his life. Although I knew there were similarities among suicides, no one could say that all of them were the same.

"He's not wearing a backpack," I said.

"Do you know he had one?"

"I would think he would. If he had water or food with him, he wouldn't hold them in his hand."

I kept looking at pictures. Finally I saw a few, not of the body, but of the trail Heinz had been walking before he fell. On the path were a shirt and a small backpack. "Look at this."

Jack took the picture. "He left them on the trail."

"Maybe he was going to eat something when he slipped and fell."

Jack didn't answer. The other possibility was just as likely: that he had put these things down before jumping to his death.

"Nothing is conclusive," I said.

"In a case like this, nothing ever is."

"You have the name of that deputy?"

"Right here."

"Maybe I'll talk to him."

"Here's the address and phone number of the sheriff's office."

I thought that maybe he would take Joseph and me up to the accident scene. "Thanks, honey."

He handed me the file. It was now officially my business.

4

Joseph and I flew to Phoenix together. I had told her a few weeks earlier of the death of Heinz Gruner, and she had said she would enjoy walking trails at Picacho Peak Park, whether we found any answers to my questions or not. We left on a cool Saturday morning in New York and arrived at Sky Harbor on a warm Saturday afternoon. A three-hour difference in time gave us a bonus of a few more hours of daylight.

The car Joseph had reserved was waiting for us, and the car rental company provided a map to get us to our hotel. I had additional maps of Arizona, Phoenix, and

Tucson, with routes marked to take us to a variety of destinations.

I also had an appointment with Deputy Sheriff Warren Gonzales. We had spoken one afternoon a couple of weeks before, and he'd told me that the place where Heinz Gruner had died was just off the highway from Phoenix to Tucson. If I called him as we left Phoenix, he would know when to meet us at the park. The trail that Heinz had taken was neither a beginner's nor an experienced hiker's path, but something in between. If we were in reasonably good shape, we would have no trouble managing the climb. Just bring extra water and wear a hat, he said.

"Water" was a word I heard often in the Southwest. We were constantly cautioned to drink *before* we became thirsty, something I'd never done before. I had brought summer clothes with me, but Joseph's habit was somewhat heavy for hot weather, and hot it was. When we awoke on Sunday morning for mass, the forecast was for ninety.

We had lunch in a restaurant that served southwestern food, and I enjoyed the spicy tang. Jack would have loved it. Joseph was hesitant, but smiled as she ate. We walked around after lunch, stopping frequently to drink our water. Joseph's meeting was scheduled for late in the afternoon, so this was the last time we would be together for a few days.

"I can see why everything is air-conditioned," Joseph said. "It must be eighty out."

A few minutes later, we came across an outdoor thermometer. "Look at that," I said, pointing.

"Ninety! I can't believe it. At home I'm sweltering at ninety. There must be something to this dry weather after all."

We stopped at several shops and looked at Navajo and Zuni pottery and jewelry. The stones were colorful, the blue of the turquoise and the bright red of the coral. A pendant of green malachite caught my eye. One could wear fabulous jewelry and never even miss precious stones.

"I think my niece may benefit from this trip," Joseph said. "She's a lovely girl and I bet she'd be thrilled to wear something so beautiful. Maybe I'll commission you to find something for her during your solo excursions in the next couple of days."

"That would be fun. I've never been much of a shopper, but these things are really different. I'm getting a kick out of just looking."

We continued for a couple of hours, then returned to the hotel. Joseph's meeting was beginning with a get-together in late afternoon, followed by a dinner. I would be on my own. After she left, I called home.

Eddie answered. "Mommy," he said excitedly, "Grandma made roast chicken and those little potatoes with bugs on them and green peas with onions. I even ate the onions, they were so good." The "bugs" were probably rosemary, one of my mother-in-law's specialties. "And she brought a cake with her." Not a word about missing his mother. Oh well, better than tears and recriminations.

41

"Sounds like you're having a great time."

"I am. Are you having a good time, too?" I had heard a little prompting in the background.

I laughed. "I'm enjoying myself a lot. Let me talk to Daddy now."

After our conversation, I talked to Jack's mother, who promised she would leave lots of good food for when I came home. Obviously, there were great advantages to having a mother-in-law in the catering business. I wondered what I would leave for my own future daughter-in-law besides my good wishes in the years to come.

I joined Joseph for mass on Monday morning, then said good-bye. I had a map to Scottsdale, a place I had been advised to visit. After breakfast, I looked at the directions and went to the parking lot with my maps and a bottle of water.

I don't spend many days the way I spent that one. Mel had given me the names of a couple of stores that I could not miss, and Joseph had authorized me to find a gift for her niece. In Scottsdale the shopping district was lined with shops, more than I had ever seen in one place. There were galleries that I sauntered through, looking at paintings and blown glass and sculptures. I saw more jewelry than I knew existed. After an hour of wandering, I felt almost giddy. Seeing so much made it harder than I had anticipated to make a decision.

Finally I took Mel's advice and drove across Goldwater Boulevard to the small store she had recommended most. I pressed the doorbell and was given entrance. The interior was small, the owner and his wife friendly and welcoming, as I had found many people to be in this part of the country. When I mentioned Mel's name, they recognized it immediately. She had called several months before to buy some gifts. Suddenly I was treated like nobility.

I was ushered into the vault, where I found the turquoise pendant that would become a gift for Joseph's niece. I also bought a silver belt buckle for Jack, hoping it wasn't too southwestern for him to wear in the city.

"What did my friend Melanie order?" I asked finally.

Husband and wife discussed it. "A card case," the wife said. "I don't have anything exactly like it, but it looked a little like this." She took out a shiny silver case with a turquoise on the front. It was beautiful.

"My mother-in-law is a caterer," I said. "I think she'd love this for her business cards." I set it down on the counter and looked at it. I am the penny-pincher in the family, as everyone knows, and I have to think about what I consider unnecessary or extravagant expenditures. Eileen was having a birthday soon. She was attractive and loved fine things. She was also responsible for some of our best eating. "I'll take it," I said, feeling somewhat breathless. I knew Jack would be pleased when he saw it. I took my credit card out of my bag and laid it on the counter, once again grateful to my husband for getting it for me at a time that I would never have considered carrying one—assuming incorrectly that I would instantly become a spendthrift.

I stayed and chatted for a while after my transaction

had been rung up. Then I took one of the store's cards in case I thought of something I just couldn't live without, not a likely event.

At the corner was a wonderful mystery bookstore. I went in and looked at the titles. I thought this might be a fine place for me to find some new writers to introduce to the students in my class on mysteries. After half an hour of browsing and chatting, I walked out with three books, looking forward to starting one when I finished the one I had brought along.

It was now after three. My shopping had been successful, and I drove back to Phoenix, avoiding the rush hour. It was late when I finally saw Joseph. She called me on the hotel phone and invited me to come down to the bar and have a drink with her and some of the participants of her conference. I had been reading and was glad for the chance to meet people and talk. The bar was filled with nuns, in and out of habit, and a handful of priests. I found Joseph and sat in the chair she had saved for me. When the waiter came, I ordered a glass of sherry.

The other nuns at the table were from different orders: a Sister of Charity, a Sister of St. Joseph, and a Dominican. The discussion was about the focus of the conference, the waning reserve of new nuns, the aging of the current nuns, and where to look for a resolution. As the conversation progressed, I could see fatigue in all the women's eyes. They were not used to staying up late; they awoke early. As soon as the first one looked at her watch and decided to leave, the party broke up.

"It sounds as though you're big on problems and short on solutions," I said to Joseph when we were in our room.

"No one expects to find a solution this week. I did, however, get some comfort from one of the discussions today. The fact that St. Stephen's has a college goes a long way toward keeping us alive. We're not just a group of aging nuns; we perform a vital service that most convents do not."

"I'm relieved to hear that." It has been a constant worry of mine that the convent would be closed down, the nuns scattered to other, more viable convents.

"Did you shop today?"

"Did I shop! Joseph, look at what I have." I opened the little boxes in my bag and showed her everything, telling her about the shop I visited last.

She drew in her breath when she saw the turquoise pendant. "This is magnificent. She will love it. What a find."

I showed her the other things and she admired them. "Nothing for yourself?"

"I don't need anything."

"That's my Chris. Oh, I am so tired. Thinking is every bit as strenuous as physical exercise. I am getting ready for bed."

The following day I drove to a few other places the AAA had marked for me. I didn't buy anything except a T-shirt for Eddie, but I took a lot of pictures. This was the second and last day of the conference. We were checking out in the morning and driving to Tucson with a stop at Picacho Peak Park. I had the file on Heinz's death with me, Deputy Gonzales's phone number, and a full tank of gas. In a way, my personal adventure would begin in the morning.

5

On Wednesday we had a large breakfast in the hotel, then packed, and checked out. A clerk assured us it would be an easy drive to Tucson.

From the parking lot, I called Deputy Gonzales on Joseph's cell phone. As the General Superior, she required one when she was away from the convent. The deputy gave me an estimate of how long it would take to drive to our meeting place. I told him to add an extra fifteen minutes—we might not drive as fast as Arizonans. He laughed and said he would do that.

Joseph drove and I navigated. Once we were on I-10 headed for Tucson, there was little for me to do. We just stayed on the road until we got off for the park. The mountain peak loomed ahead of us for half an hour, on one side of the road or the other, before we reached our exit. The shape was distinctive, and I hoped we wouldn't have to hike to the top. My guidebook pegged it at almost thirty-four hundred feet. I took my wallet out to pay the entrance fee as we approached the park.

Just beyond the kiosk was a sheriff's car. We parked at the side of the road in front of it and got out as the door opened and a uniformed man put his hat on and joined us.

"Morning, ladies. I'm Deputy Warren Gonzales. Happy to meet you." He extended his hand and we shook it in turn, introducing ourselves.

"Hope you had an easy drive," he said.

We assured him we had.

"Tell you what I think we should do. You've got the map of the park." We had just been given it. "This is the parking area we'll go to." He circled it. "We can leave our cars there and start to climb. You ladies got good shoes on?"

I was wearing sneakers, and Joseph had sturdy shoes. Deputy Gonzales looked at them and frowned.

"I'll be fine," Joseph said. "Shall we follow you?"

"If you wouldn't mind."

There were several parking areas, each of them near a trail with the difficulty marked. Deputy Gonzales drove slowly, then signaled his turn. Before he left the car, he put a sun shield in the front of his window. We hadn't thought to buy one, so Joseph parked with the front of the car facing away from the sun. We each took a bottle of water along, to the approval of the deputy.

"OK, let me show you where we're going." He opened his map of the park, put an X in the parking area where we stood, and traced the trail with his finger. "As I remember, the body was about up here." He pointed. "Not on the trail but down off the side of it. We won't be able to get to that exact point, but I can show you

47

where we found his backpack. That your husband we faxed the file to, Ms. Bennett?"

"Lt. Jack Brooks. That's my husband. I have the file with me. We've both looked it over."

"Real nice fellow, your husband. So you have an idea what I found when I got here that day. OK, if you're ready, let's start up the trail."

He led, stopping from time to time to let us rest. As we went, he gave us some history. The Civil War battle of Picacho Pass had taken place here in the spring of 1862, half a century before Arizona became a state. The sun was high now, the sky an amazing bright blue without a hint of clouds. I was glad I had thought to take along a straw hat. Without it, I would have been in bad shape. I was concerned about Joseph's comfort, but she didn't seem any worse off than I was. Deputy Gonzales, a trim man with a touch of gray, mopped his face once or twice, but apparently had a pair of legs used to hard work.

The scenery was beautiful. Deputy Gonzales told us that in the spring the entire mountainside was covered with wildflowers. "Real pretty," he said. "People come from all over to see it."

"How long have you been with the sheriff's department, Deputy Gonzales?" I asked.

"'Bout twenty-five years. And I'd appreciate it if you'd call me Warren. We're pretty casual here in Arizona."

"Thank you. I'm Chris."

He gave me a smile. "We're almost there."

48

We had been hiking for almost half an hour, and I was glad to hear that the end was in sight. I would have given anything for a gallon of ice water, but my quart bottle was keeping me in good shape. As I looked left and right, I could see the occasional hiker on another path. Two people came downhill as we went up, and we moved aside to let them through. They were young and cheerful and told us it was beautiful up ahead.

"OK, ladies," Warren called down to us. He had gotten some distance from us and now he stood and waited as we climbed more slowly. "Just around this bend."

We joined him and turned the corner, leaving the trail we had covered out of our field of vision. Another minute and he stopped.

"Just about here," he said. "The backpack was about where I'm standing. Down there," he pointed to a steep incline, "right where that stand of trees is—that's where we saw his body."

"So the trees stopped his fall," Joseph said.

"Looked that way, ma'am. He'd probably turned over a couple of times on the way down, slid some, grabbed onto scrub, but couldn't stop his fall, then went into the trees."

"How do you know he grabbed onto anything?" I asked.

"His hands were scratched, kinda bloody if I remember."

That would mean he hadn't committed suicide, I thought. Of course, after having jumped or hurled himself down, he might have changed his mind or instinctively tried to stop his fall.

"I don't remember seeing any comments about his hands in the autopsy report," I said.

"Haven't read it for twenty years. The ME was pretty sure it was an accident, so maybe he wasn't as thorough as he could've been. I don't think going down the slope is a very good idea, ladies."

I had to agree. I took some pictures of the slope, the stand of trees, the trail, and put my camera away. "What kind of trees are those?" I asked.

"They're mesquites. Lots of them in this part of the country. They use 'em to flavor barbecue, and they make furniture out of the good pieces. Beautiful wood when it's sanded and oiled."

They didn't look very beautiful now, but rather scraggly.

"Over there, that tree that's green from the roots up, that's a *palo verde*. Means 'green stick' and that's what it is. Even the trunk stays green." He turned to me. "What is the purpose of your seeing this place?"

"I knew him from high school. His death destroyed not only his life but his parents' lives as well. His father died of a heart attack about a year afterward, and his mother had a stroke that's left her with difficulty walking. The fear they both had is that he killed himself."

"It's possible," Warren said, "but I don't believe it. You can see how hot it is right now at the beginning of May. My recollection is that he died on or about the fifth, Cinco de Mayo."

"What's that?" Joseph asked.

"Ah, a great day in Mexican history, Sister: the day General Zaragoza won the battle of Puebla in 1862 after Maximilian was executed. If not for that, we could have had a French country south of the border."

Joseph smiled. "Thank you. Please go on."

"Let's see. I was about to say that May can get pretty hot here, over a hundred sometimes. I expect he wasn't prepared for the heat and the dryness. Could've been dehydrated, gotten dizzy maybe, lost his balance."

"That's what I'd like to find out," I said. "I'd like to be able to tell his mother it was an accident. It won't make her a happy woman, but it will ease her conscience if she knows it wasn't suicide."

"Tough to prove one way or another. I got my gut feelings to go by, but that won't convince this poor fellow's mother."

"I know."

"Which tree was his body up against?" Joseph asked.

"The one in the middle. It was in better shape twenty years ago. See that moss hanging from those branches? That's in the process of killing the tree. Next time you come, it may not be here."

"That's a saguaro, isn't it?" I asked, pointing to a large cactus whose arms stretched up and out.

"Oh yeah. You'll see a lot of 'em in Arizona. Won't see 'em much elsewhere."

"They're really something."

"I'm sure you know that suicide is a very touchy issue in the Catholic Church," Joseph said. "Priests often

51

officiate at funerals for suicide victims on the assumption that they may have changed their minds when it was too late to save themselves. This could be one of those times."

"Which makes it harder to figure out what happened," I added. "Was anything found near the body, Warren? Water or food or any piece of clothing?"

"Nothing that I remember. It was pretty messy. There are animals—"

"I know," I said, cutting him off. I didn't want to think about the close-up pictures I had seen.

"Was the backpack open or closed?" Joseph asked.

"Closed, I think. Packed kind of neat. Had his ID, Social Security card, some pictures of his parents, a driver's license."

"Anything else?"

"That should be in the file," Warren said.

"Do you have the name and address of the people who found him?"

"That's in the file," I said. "It was a local couple, people who lived in Tucson."

"Then maybe we can find them. I think it would be instructive to hear what they say."

"Don't know if they're still around after twenty years," Warren said, "but you can give it a try. I can't think of a better place to live than Tucson myself. Lots of folks feel that way."

I smiled. Then I took a last look around. I asked Warren if I might take a picture of him, just as a memento. He gave me a grin and stood up straight while I pointed and shot. I promised to send him a copy.

"We done here?" he asked as I dropped the camera in my purse.

"I think so," I said.

"Get any answers?"

"Just a few more questions."

"Well, in my business, that's considered progress. Let's head back down before we melt."

6

We said our good-byes in the parking lot. I promised Warren I would be in touch with him if I learned anything new. He said it had been a pleasure taking us up the trail.

We got back on the interstate and continued toward Tucson. The traffic picked up as we drove and the speed limit dropped. We exited at Broadway and Congress, two parallel streets, each one-way in the opposite direction. Our hotel was close to the highway; we were soon registered and in our room.

We had talked about the case all the way down from Picacho Peak. It was the scratches on Heinz's hands that concerned us both. Had instinct overcome his conscious desire to kill himself, or had he fallen and attempted to stop himself all the way down to the stand of trees?

We decided to try to find the couple who had discovered the body. In the hotel room I located their name, which was in the file, and found them in the telephone directory, although the address was different from the one they had given twenty years before. I made the call and spoke to a girl who said she was their daughter. Her parents would not be home before five thirty. I promised to call back.

Meanwhile, we were very hungry, so we went downstairs and ate some lunch. By the time we finished, it was late afternoon. We found out we were quite close to the Museum of Art and Old Town, two places on our visiting list. The museum closed at four, so that was out of the question, but we walked across a footbridge that spanned the two streets, finding ourselves in a large plaza with a fountain in the center and a beautiful old courthouse with a mosaic dome at the far end. We continued across the plaza till we came to a street, crossed it, and found Old Town. It was a low historic building filled with shops selling pottery, jewelry, and art objects from the Southwest.

We walked around until we both agreed that our climb earlier in the day had made us ache too much to continue, so we returned to the hotel. I had brought *The New York Times* along from Phoenix and we shared it as we rested. A little before six, I called the number listed for Bradley Tower, the husband who had found the backpack.

Mrs. Tower answered. I explained who I was and why I was calling.

"You mean that poor fellow who fell down the mountainside? That must have been twenty years ago."

"That's the one. I wonder if we could get together and

talk, Mrs. Tower. Your husband, too. I know that young man's mother and I'm trying to get as much information about his death as I can."

She left the phone and had a long conversation with her husband. "We could come down to your hotel tomorrow," she said. "How would ten o'clock in the morning be?"

"That would be great. We'll be downstairs in the lobby. My companion is a nun, so you'll recognize her right away."

We left it at that. I called home and had a quick chat with Jack. Eddie was sleeping and all was well. When I was off the phone, I found I was so tired that all I wanted was to get some sleep myself. I got no complaints from Joseph. She was already getting her nightshirt out of the drawer.

We returned to the hotel before ten the next morning and took chairs facing an entrance. The Towers arrived punctually, Mrs. Tower's face lighting up when she spotted Joseph.

I brought them over to the arrangement of chairs and a sofa around a table and we introduced ourselves.

"Before we begin," Bradley Tower said, "I'd like to know how you found us."

I explained that I had the file of Heinz Gruner's accident, and their names and old address were in it.

He looked troubled. "You can just put your hands on a criminal file anytime you want to?"

"It's not a criminal file," I said. "It's a police file of

55

the accidental death of a boy I went to high school with. You and your wife reported it. As a matter of fact, I didn't get the file myself. My husband is a lieutenant in the New York Police Department. But nothing in that file is sealed."

"I see."

"Is there a problem?"

He and his wife exchanged a glance. I suspected they'd had some conversation about this.

"I think we're OK," he said. "What did you want to know?"

"Anything you can remember about finding the body. Were you going uphill or downhill when you spotted it?"

"Downhill," Mary Ann Tower said. "We came around the bend and I looked down the slope and there it was."

"She was pretty upset," her husband said. "Not that I wasn't. But she kind of got faint and I had to steady her."

"Did you go down to the body?" I asked.

"Mary Ann wouldn't hear of it. I wanted to, in case the poor guy was still alive."

"You could tell he wasn't," Mary Ann said. "Even from that distance, you could see the animals had gotten to him. It was awful."

"So we knew it hadn't just happened."

"What did you do? Did you have a cell phone?"

He laughed. "That was twenty years ago. There weren't any cell phones then. We hiked down the mountain and went to the tollbooth and reported it. The gal there called a ranger and the police, and a deputy came awhile later. We hiked back up with him to be sure he went to the right place. The ranger led the way."

"A lot of hiking for one day," I said.

"You bet. But we were in good shape then, right, Mary Ann?"

She smiled. "Those were the days."

"I understand there was a backpack on the trail."

"Right. I didn't open it. I figured it was his."

"Funny that no one found it before you did."

"There aren't always a lot of people on that trail. What time of year did that happen?" he asked his wife.

"May."

"Right. May seventh. They figured he'd fallen a couple of days earlier, Cinco de Mayo, fifth of May. I remember it was real hot, too hot to climb, but we'd been planning that for a while."

"Was there anything that you saw that struck you as strange?"

"The whole thing was strange. I'd never seen a dead body before in my life. I see how he could've fallen, but he shouldn't have. He didn't have his backpack on, so he wasn't weighed down. I couldn't figure what made him fall."

"He was from the East," I said. "He may have gotten dehydrated. You said yourself it was hot."

"That's what I said," Mary Ann declared. "The heat got to him, he felt dizzy, and he fell."

"You mean he put his backpack down nice and neat by the side of the trail and then toppled over?" Brad sounded scornful. "I could almost believe it if he had the backpack on. It could've unbalanced him."

"Well, we'll never know," his wife said dismissively.

"Did you go up that same trail that you came down?"

"Sure," Brad said.

Sister Joseph leaned forward. "Didn't you come upon the backpack on your way up?"

The couple looked at each other. "I didn't see it," Mary Ann said.

"Neither did I."

"Could you have missed it?"

Brad shook his head. "I don't think so. That's not a wide trail. Even if we weren't looking, one of us would've been sure to kick it as we went by."

"Are you suggesting that the backpack wasn't there when we went up and someone put it there while we were coming down?" Mary Ann looked deeply concerned.

"It's a possibility," Joseph said. "Did the police ask you which way you were walking when you spotted the body?"

"I don't remember," Brad said, looking at Mary Ann.

"I was awfully upset. I didn't go back up with them when the deputy came. I wasn't thinking too clearly. It was such an awful sight."

"So you may not have been asked," Joseph said thoughtfully.

"What are you getting at?" Brad asked. "They said it was an accident. It looked like an accident. You think it was something else?" He seemed reluctant to use the word that we were probably all thinking.

"We can't say at this moment. Chris and I both read the file and neither of us noticed whether you were asked which direction you were hiking when you found the body. Maybe it didn't occur to the deputy to ask. It was twenty years ago; he was young and less experienced. I wouldn't be surprised if that was the first time he'd encountered a body."

"But what you're saying is important," Brad said. "Everyone assumed this guy died by accident. You're saying it could have been murder."

"I'm not saying that. There are several possibilities. Perhaps some hiker reached the backpack before you and took it off the trail to a secluded place to see what was in it. Maybe he was interested in finding the owner."

"Or stealing what was in it," Mary Ann said.

"We can't exclude that. I just wanted to point out that the disappearance and reappearance of the backpack doesn't necessarily add up to murder."

"Sorry I jumped the gun," Brad said. "I wish someone had thought of this twenty years ago. It's kind of late in the game to be discovering new facts."

"It's not too late," I said. "This young man's mother wants to know what happened. If we can find out, we'll be doing her a service."

Brad looked at his watch. "Honey, we really have to go." He turned to Joseph and me. "Will you let us know what happens? I mean, if you find out that there was some kind of foul play, we'd really like to know."

"I have your name and number," I said. "You'll hear from me. It may be awhile."

"Hey, after twenty years, what's another couple of weeks?"

We all shook hands, and they left. Joseph and I decided to have some lunch in the hotel as we were driving down to the San Xavier Mission that afternoon. Sitting at the table after we had ordered, we talked about this disquieting new piece of information.

"Obviously," Joseph said, "the original questioning of the Towers was deficient. It's interesting that neither of them thought anything was unusual about not seeing the backpack on the way up and finding it on the way down."

"They were upset. I'm sure they weren't thinking clearly. And no one had reason to suspect anything besides an accident." I drank half a glass of ice water. "I wonder if Heinz had a car with him. The rangers must check the parking lots in the evening. If a car is left—"

"It puts up a red flag. That didn't happen."

"He might have thumbed a ride from his starting point."

"That must have been the case."

I pulled my notebook out and made a note. If Heinz had rented a car, the company would have had Heinz's home address and would have contacted the Gruners when he didn't return it. Or the sheriff's department would have intervened. Thinking about it, I barely noticed when the food arrived.

"It doesn't make sense that he drove," I said, putting the notebook on the table. "Are you convinced that someone took the backpack and returned it, Joseph?"

"I am. It's possible that the backpack was taken as early as May fifth and was returned on the seventh after the Towers passed the spot going up."

"Why would someone take it? Why would they return it?"

"They took it to see if something in it was worth stealing. They returned it to identify the body."

"Which means the Towers weren't the first ones to see the body or the backpack."

"It still doesn't add up to murder, Chris, if that's what you're thinking."

"It *is* what I'm thinking even if I'm taking giant leaps here. In fact—" I put my fork down as ideas flooded my mind. "What if Heinz drove to Picacho Peak with someone else in the other person's car?"

"That would answer some questions we've just asked."

"Like what became of the car."

"Then it could have been a murder that developed from hitchhiking," Joseph said.

"How awful. But you're right. That would make it a crime of opportunity."

"And no way to trace whoever drove the car and pushed Heinz off the edge of the path."

She was right. Two men drive into the park, pay the entrance fee, park at the base of a trail, and start up together. They have just met, perhaps an hour or two earlier. They are talking, enjoying each other's company. They walk the trail, come to the fateful spot, and something happens.

"But once again," Joseph said, "even if we insert this additional person into the mix, the man driving the car, it could still have been an accident. The other person felt he wasn't able to scale the slope to help him. He panics, grabs the backpack, and goes back down. A day or two later, he returns with the backpack. Do you have the file with you, Chris?"

"Right here." I took it out of the canvas tote bag.

"I'm sure I remember seeing a list of the contents of the backpack. What was in it?"

I rummaged through the file. "No money," I said. "But I think there was a wallet in his pant pocket. A hat, just as I thought. One unopened bottle of water."

"He could have drunk another bottle and discarded it."

"Right. Half a sandwich, two ice packs to keep food cold, both thawed. A hand towel, a case for eyeglasses. His glasses were near the body. A small transistor radio. He probably wanted to hear the news or some music. Look at this. A postcard to his parents. Had no stamp on it. He was going to mail it when he got some stamps. That doesn't sound like he was planning to kill himself. Kleenex, hand wipes. That's about it." I sat looking at the list.

"Do you see what's missing?"

I went down the list a second time. "Nothing pops out."

"Clothes."

"Of course," I said. "He had no extra clothes with him. He had them in a suitcase or a larger backpack."

"And he left it in the car he came in. I think this tells us that there was a car and driver."

"Or that he had a room in a hotel somewhere—but that means the hotel would have called his parents' number looking for him to pay the bill. Mrs. Gruner didn't say anything about that, but I can ask her. And if he was staying in a hotel, he needed transportation to get to the park."

"What this says to me is that it's unlikely he committed suicide," Joseph said. "He had to have traveled with clothes. If the clothes were left in a hotel, why didn't they turn up?"

I returned to the file. There was no mention of anyone looking for a hotel room. "I'm going to call Deputy Gonzales," I said. "I'll be right back."

I found a pay phone and dialed the number. Gonzales answered immediately.

"Warren, this is Chris Bennett."

"Well, hello there. You and the sister still thinking about that death in the park?"

"We are, and we have some questions. Do you know if Heinz Gruner was registered at a hotel at the time of his death or the night before?"

"Well, we did some digging on that, called a bunch of places, came up with nothing."

"Sister Joseph and I just realized that he had no clothes with him except for what he was wearing. We

63

read the list of the contents of the backpack and all it had was a sandwich and some Kleenex and things like that."

"Young folks don't always travel with a suitcase, you know," the deputy said. "They rough it."

"He didn't have a toothbrush. He didn't have a change of socks or underwear."

"You're right about that. But we never recovered any."

"There's something else." I had made a split-second decision to tell him what we had learned that morning. "We spoke to that couple who found the body, the Towers. They were on their way *down* the mountain when they spotted the body and the backpack."

"OK."

"They had gone up the same way earlier in the day. I'm not surprised they didn't see the body because of the angle, but they didn't see the *backpack* on the way up."

There was silence from the deputy. Then he said, "They were coming down when they saw the body and on the way up they missed the backpack?"

"Yes."

"Interesting."

"They couldn't have missed it if it was there, Warren. The trail is narrow. Even if they were looking away, they would have kicked it as they went by. We think the backpack was taken after the accident and brought back just before the Towers came down the mountain."

"I suppose that could have happened," Warren said.

"Someone could've seen it, thought it had money, taken it away with him to check, and brought it back when he'd taken what he wanted out of it. Could've been a piece of jewelry in there that the fellow didn't want to wear in the heat, like a ring."

"That's what we were thinking," I said, not wanting to get involved in a discussion of possible homicide.

"Well, that's interesting. It's so long ago, I don't remember whether I asked those folks if they were going up or down, and if it's not in the file, they didn't volunteer it. But I agree with you that because of the curve of the trail, you'd see the body coming down easier than going up."

"I just wanted you to know what we found out."

"My recollection is the father flew down and identified the body, and we gave him the backpack and whatever we had. There was a wallet in his pocket, as I remember."

"I saw that, yes. Well, thanks for your time." I went back to the table and told Joseph what I had learned.

"So no suitcase, no clothes, no big backpack. I'm sure the parents were too distraught to think about such mundane things."

"And as far as the police were concerned, young people just roughed it and didn't bother changing their clothes. Or using a toothbrush," I added.

"I think we've learned something valuable," Joseph said. "Whether the companion took the backpack or a third party did, I'm convinced there was another container of possessions that he left somewhere rather than carry it as he climbed. And the place was very likely the car he came in."

"OK," I said. The check had been dropped on the table in my absence. "We've accomplished something. Let's go look at that mission."

7

Everyone knew of the San Xavier Mission, which was on a reservation not far south of our hotel. The drive was barely twenty minutes. I took the wheel and Joseph kept her eyes peeled for the first sight of it, which turned out to be quite dramatic.

"Look," she said, leaning forward. "Over to the right, that magnificent white structure rising out of the desert."

I could hear the excitement in her voice. I glanced to my right and saw it, a white dome atop a long, low white building. A moment later we passed a sign that we were entering the reservation, and soon I came to the exit. We drove through farmland, finally approaching the mission, which stood just beyond a wide-open space with parking along the left side. We got out of the car and began to walk through the dusty open area. Off to our right, well beyond the building, was a small hill with a large cross planted on the top. Several people were climbing toward it.

We entered the church and went into the dark interior. Old wooden pews, smoothed by age and use, flanked a center aisle in the narrow sanctuary. Candles burned ahead of us in the nave. The atmosphere was hushed. In the left transept was a statue of San Xavier, reclining under a coverlet adorned with tokens representing desired miracles. These tiny arms and legs and hearts had been pinned in place by visitors.

We made a slow round of the church, then left to visit the museum in a wing off to the right. There we found historical pictures and artifacts going back hundreds of years. The building had been started by Father Eusebio Kino in 1700, but most of it had been constructed by Franciscans and completed almost a hundred years later. Exiting behind the building, we walked through a beautiful courtyard with flowering plants and tropical trees.

"What a wonderful place," Joseph said, "and built by Franciscans. If I saw nothing else on this trip, I would consider it successful to have come here."

On the way back, we stopped and bought candles that we took inside to light. Whenever I have the opportunity, I light three, one for each of my parents and one for Aunt Meg.

Outside in the hot sun, we decided to take a hike up to the cross.

"I think we'll both be a few pounds lighter when we get back," Joseph said.

"And more muscular. I feel every step in my legs."

We took it slowly, spending close to an hour on the hill. Many of the people around us spoke Spanish. Others looked as though they might be Indians from nearby reservations.

Back at ground level, we sauntered toward the car, the late-afternoon sun beating down on us. A priest walked by and stopped to talk to Joseph. I left them and continued toward the car, which was as hot as an oven. I opened the windows and turned on the air conditioner till it was cool enough to close up. Joseph was striding toward the car. She got in, thanking me for cooling it off.

I drove back to the hotel, Joseph turning to look at the mission for the last time.

We ate at a well-known Mexican restaurant a few blocks from the hotel. It was pleasant enough that we could eat outside in the garden. In the desert, I learned, the nights were cool most of the year, affording relief after the hot days. The food was different from any I had ever eaten. Unsweetened chocolate was used as a flavor with the meat, and skeptical as I was when I placed my order, it was delicious. I knew Jack would love it.

"This was certainly a successful day," Joseph said. "We learned some important things connected to your investigation and I satisfied a desire I have had for more than twenty years. We couldn't ask for much more."

"But I have much more to find out. Now that I suspect there was another person present when Heinz fell, I know I have to continue digging into this. I've been wondering whether Heinz traveled to Arizona alone. He might have come with someone from school."

"His airline ticket was missing. It may have been in the missing suitcase."

"Or among the things that were stolen out of the backpack."

"Good thought," Joseph said. "Twenty years ago you didn't need picture ID to travel. Any man could have posed as Heinz Gruner and gotten a free flight back to wherever he came from. I think you have many questions to ask his mother, Chris."

I agreed. "I hope she doesn't find it too stressful."

"She'll overcome it. This has been the agony of her life. She wants answers, most of all to the question of whether her son committed suicide. While it seemed a likely possibility a few days ago, it doesn't anymore."

"It's hard to imagine anyone would have wanted to kill him," I said. "He wasn't a bully, he kept to himself, he was pleasant enough even if he wasn't outgoing. I know so little about him, it's hard to know where to begin."

"You know little about any of the victims whose deaths you have investigated. They come to you out of the blue with no history, no known friends or business associates. You learn all that when you look into their deaths. You're ahead of the game here. You remember this person and you've met his mother. That puts you two giant steps ahead of most of your other inquiries."

I had begun writing notes to myself as she spoke, things I wanted to ask Mrs. Gruner, other things I wanted to find out from Heinz's college. They might have a record of the people in his dormitory, especially those whose rooms were near his. It made sense that he would live near friends he had made in previous years.

"I'm going to have to contact his college," I said. "I'm sure Mrs. Gruner will remember where he went. The college has to know what happened to Heinz. A catastrophe like that doesn't happen often."

"That's a good start. When you start putting out feelers, more things will pop up. Old acquaintances will surface. Not that I'm telling you something you don't already know."

We had managed to talk all through dinner. Now we sipped our coffee, hearing voices and laughter from nearby tables. It was so peaceful here, it almost seemed wrong to be talking about a possible murder.

We drove to the Desert Museum after breakfast on Friday morning. It opened early, and we were both early birds. The trip itself was worth the drive. The road wound through mountains covered with saguaros and other cactus plants that were beginning to look as familiar to me as oaks and maples and sycamores in the East.

We received maps of the paths through the museum grounds as we entered. We knew there was too much to cover in one morning, so we elected to go to our left toward the hummingbird aviary, and after that, to the large aviary. In between we saw the plants and trees of the Sonoran Desert, mesquite and *palo verde* trees that were green from the ground up to the top, like those Deputy Gonzales had pointed out on the mountain.

There were numerous varieties of chollas and agaves, beautiful golden barrels, and cactus plants that looked like works of art—the way they crept here and there, coiled around themselves, and occasionally bloomed.

"I am done in," Joseph said as we neared the main building after wending our way along a mile of paths. "I think the other half of this wonderful place will have to wait for another visit."

"If I can persuade Jack to come, you'll have to join us. I think he would just eat up everything we've seen and want more."

We went inside and looked around the gift shop, enjoying the air-conditioning. I bought a small jar of Sonoran honey and a T-shirt for Eddie. By the time I finished this trip, his summer wardrobe would be complete. Joseph picked up some honey, too, a larger jar to share with the nuns who breakfasted with her. Then we hiked to our car and drove back to the city.

"I must say I like being a tourist," Joseph said as we sat under the trees in the courtyard of Old Town, sipping lemonade and eating southwestern salads. "I've become quite adept at it in very few days. Do you think we'll have time to visit the convent?"

I looked at my watch. "Of course we have time. We can visit the museum and then drive out there."

Joseph opened a map of Tucson and located the convent she'd heard about. "It's quite far east. It may take us half an hour or more to get there."

"That's what we're here for," I said. "We'll get there."

71

After lunch we walked through several of the Old Town shops, coming out near the entrance to the Museum of Art. We stopped in their gift shop first, where everything was made by southwestern artists. I picked up a few things for Eddie, Jack, and my mother-in-law, happy that I could give them beautiful and unusual gifts one would never see on the East Coast.

Then we took a swing through the museum to see the new exhibit. The afternoon was half over when we finished. I took the wheel and Joseph guided me east and north, giving us a new part of the city to admire. There were hills and canyons in the northeast, saguaros growing everywhere, the scenery wonderful.

We reached the convent, which appeared to be empty, the church locked, a Spanish-speaking gardener unable to answer our questions. What Joseph wanted to see were the Stations of the Cross spread on the hill beyond the buildings. We walked up to the first two, then came down again. It was getting late, and we had a long drive back to the hotel. This had been our last day in Arizona, and we had packed more into the week than I had expected.

As I had promised and Jack had insisted, I took Joseph out to a memorable dinner. I think by then I had fallen in love with Tucson and was hoping to arrange to get our family out here. I had been amazed by the amount of art I saw, not just for sale in shops and galleries, but also along the roads we traveled, in the restaurants, and out-of-doors, where people passed it and appreciated it daily. By contrast, our lovely town of Oakwood in New York seemed dull and colorless. It needed a few murals, I thought, or some handsome pieces of sculpture, or an artistic bench one could sit on while contemplating a clear blue sky. Not much chance that we would ever achieve anything so lofty, but it was nice to dream.

In the morning, we drove to the airport, returned the car, checked in, and went through security. I had never felt so sad at leaving a place that I hardly knew. When we were at our gate with time to spare, I stood at the large window and looked at the bluest sky I had ever seen, at the mountains that turned gold and pink and purple at sunset.

"This was a wonderful trip," Joseph said at my side. "I know I will miss this place."

"So will I. I think I finally know what love at first sight means."

"I thought that applied to relationships between men and women."

"It may do that also. Look at that sky, Joseph. Look at those mountains. I've never seen anything like it. Imagine waking up every day to those mountains."

Joseph was silent. A moment later our flight was called. Half an hour after that, I saw the city and the mountains for the last time as we headed north and east. I felt very lucky.

8

For the first time, I found it hard to get back to my routine. I haven't visited many places—although our trip to Israel a couple of years before was as good as traveling gets—but the Southwest had worked its charm on me, and I continued to feel its pull for several days after my return. It was May in the East, too, but the sky was duller, the air chillier, my daily tasks more of a burden. I kept this to myself while talking about the trip and telling Jack how much he and Eddie would enjoy Arizona.

Sunday was my buffer day, time to get back to normal, performing the mundane but necessary tasks of life like doing laundry. After mass, Jack took us all out to a buffet brunch, including my cousin Gene, who lives in a residence for retarded adults here in town. Grandma Brooks was already back home in Brooklyn, having left me enough meals and desserts for several days. That lessened the impact of running a household again, and I expressed my gratitude to her in the afternoon after we returned to the house and Eddie and Gene went outside to play.

"You want me to apply for chief of police in a small town in Arizona?" Jack asked with a twinkle after I got off the phone.

"Wouldn't that be nice. But I'm not ready for that yet. I'd miss Joseph and the nuns. And what would I do without Mel across the street?"

"Just askin'. You haven't talked about Mrs. Gruner's son."

"We learned some interesting things, Jack." I walked to the window to check on the boys, who were more than thirty years apart in physical age. They were sitting at the patio table and playing some game. I came back and told him our theory that Heinz had made the climb with another person who had a car parked at the base of the trail.

"That's new. I looked through that file before I gave it to you and nothing like that was even hinted at. The guy was thought to be alone and it was a simple case of falling off the trail."

"Maybe not so simple." I told him about our meeting with the Towers, about the backpack that wasn't there and then was.

"So nobody thought to ask. That's the trouble with young, inexperienced guys."

"No one expects a fall on a mountain to be a homicide," I said, defending Gonzales's handling of the case.

"But the question of luggage, of a return plane ticket . . . the deputy should've asked. Somebody should've asked. I suppose the parents were too overwhelmed to think about things like that."

"I'm going to call Rimson College tomorrow," I said. Maddie had left a message with Jack with the name while I was gone. "I know it's a long time ago, but I bet they know the names of the students who were on his corridor in the dorm or who shared his room. Someone will remember that he went to Arizona after exams. And maybe someone will remember that he went with a friend."

"You going to talk to his mother about this?"

"Not yet. I don't want to say anything that will make her feel worse. When I have something substantial, maybe I'll sit down with her."

"Well, you're doing good, Chris. You picked up a crucial piece of information that they let slide."

Something banged outside the house and Jack dashed out to see what damage had been done. I smiled and went to the kitchen to make some lemonade for my family.

Monday was the return of normality. Jack went off to New York to be a cop and Eddie went to school, leaving me with my empty house, the Heinz Gruner file, and a shopping list that would have to be filled by late afternoon. My mind was far from shopping lists. I called information and got a phone number for Rimson College in Illinois. I knew colleges were reluctant to give out information on students and former students; still, it was a small place well out of the New York metropolitan area, and people might be more forthcoming.

When my household duties were finished, I made the call. The first person to answer switched me to the registrar's office. We had a conversation of about five minutes during which she told me she was unable to divulge the kind of information I'd requested. Another minute and she agreed to let me speak to someone in a supervisory position. When a second woman answered, I restated my story and request.

"Twenty years ago," she mused. "Those would still be paper records. They'd be in storage, and I don't have the authority to get that file."

I tried to impress her with the importance of my mission. "If this young man was murdered, it's important to bring the killer to justice."

"Do you know that he was murdered?"

"I don't. But I do know that new information has been uncovered and it conflicts with the police report at the time of his death."

"Why doesn't the police department give us a call? I'm sure we'd have no difficulty responding to them."

"Ma'am, is there a dean who's been around since the date of this student's death?"

"Let me see." She left the phone while I hoped she considered my question seriously. When she came back, she said, "We do have a dean of students here who's been with the college for a long time. He wasn't a dean back then, but I know he taught here for several years before his appointment. Would you like to talk to him?"

"Very much."

"I'll connect you."

The next person I spoke to was the dean's secretary. A moment later the dean himself came on the line.

"Dean Hershey."

"Good morning, Dean Hershey. My name is Christine

77

Bennett." I stated my case from the beginning and never got to the end.

"Heinz Gruner," he interrupted. "Yes, of course I remember his death. A terrible tragedy. He was a gifted student. It happened somewhere in the Southwest, didn't it?"

"Yes, it did. Near Tucson, Arizona."

"Heinz was a student of mine. I taught history, and he was a history major."

I almost cheered. I continued my story, adding that I had been in touch with Mrs. Gruner, who lived not far from me. When I came to the end, I asked if he would assist me in trying to find out exactly what had happened on that mountain in Arizona.

"I will do that, Miss Bennett. I knew Heinz and I liked him. He would have made a fine scholar. His goal was to teach, and I couldn't think of a better career for him. What can I do to help?"

I outlined the information I wanted, and the dean promised to put a researcher on the job immediately. He would report back to me and let me know what he had before he mailed it to me. I had the presence of mind to get his office extension before we finished our conversation. I didn't want to go through another set of hurdles if I needed to call him again.

Having achieved more than I'd hoped, I took my shopping list and went back to the homely tasks that would keep my home and family going.

Late in the day Dean Hershey called me back. "I have

everything you asked for, Miss Bennett, including a sketch of the dormitory corridor he lived on. The occupants of every room are named, and there's a list of the most recent addresses the college has. Some are as old as graduation, but many of the men have been generous donors. I have their current addresses."

"That will be very helpful, Dean Hershey. I can't thank you enough."

"All I ask of you is that you let me know the outcome of your sleuthing. I've thought for twenty years that that poor boy slipped and fell to his death, and that was bad enough. But if some person caused his death, I want to know about it."

"I'll tell you whatever I learn."

"Thank you. I'm overnighting the package. You should have it by noon tomorrow."

I called Joseph to tell her the news.

"I'm so glad you called, Chris," she said, sounding harried. "I returned to such a mess, I couldn't believe my eyes. Unanswered phone calls, a washing machine that has died of old age, Harold the gardener suddenly taken ill. I thought I was a good planner, but apparently I need to go back to planning school."

I commiserated and then told her my news.

"What luck! A dean who actually taught that young man. Of course he's interested in the outcome. It sounds as though you'll be happily busy for days to come."

"I'd certainly rather be busy talking to Heinz's old friends than shopping for a washing machine. I hope Harold is all right."

"It sounds like his annual back trouble. We'll cope. Be sure to call with news."

Before Jack came home, I got on the computer and found Rimson College's website. It was one of those fine old liberal arts colleges that specialized in English and history, languages and literature. It had both men and women students, but they had the choice of living in either separate or mixed dormitories. Heinz had opted to live with male students.

I looked at the current year's curriculum. If you were a student of American or European history, it was a fine place to study. The members of the faculty were listed with photos and bios. One had won a Pulitzer Prize some years before; another had been a Rhodes Scholar. Several had had Fulbrights. I was impressed with their credentials.

The pictures of the campus showed green grass and mostly old buildings, although two new ones were highlighted, a library of glass and steel overlooking a waterfall and a cafeteria near the dormitories. I thought how wonderful it would be to study in a place like that, how conducive to learning such a campus would be.

I made note of the professors who had been teaching there the longest in the hope that some of them might remember Heinz. The English professor who had won the Pulitzer had been there for more than thirty years; a history professor had also been on the faculty that long. One of the younger history professors had graduated from Rimson about the time that Heinz would have, had he lived. That might be a fruitful source.

80

All in all, I felt I was moving forward. Jack agreed when he came home.

"That's a stroke of luck, finding a dean who knew the guy personally. It makes him an ally."

"It really does. He's overnighting the stuff." I told him about the website, the beautiful pictures, and the fine curriculum.

"You check out the tuition?" my practical husband asked.

"I was afraid to. Whatever it is now, it'll be a lot more when Eddie's ready for college. But it would be nice for him to go to such a beautiful place."

"Looks like I better study for the captain's exam or think about private practice." He had gone to law school and passed the bar since I met him.

"Do what you enjoy doing," I said. "When the time comes, we'll find the money."

"Said by a real optimist."

"You bet." I kissed his cheek. He had given me the same advice many times.

The package from Dean Hershey arrived at eleven. I had waited nervously for the doorbell since breakfast. I brought it in and sat down at the dining room table, which we used far more for spreading out work than for eating. I slit the envelope and pulled out a stack of paper topped with a formal letter from the dean. Then I started turning pages.

Near the top of the pile was the dormitory information, a sketch of a corridor with numbered rooms on each side. The page after that listed the occupants of each room with a name, address, phone number, and e-mail address if the college had it. A third page showed an entering picture or a graduation picture for each boy. The picture of Heinz was exactly as I remembered him. I laid the sketch, the list, and the photos on the table side by side and began to go down the list of names. One of them sounded familiar: Herbert Fallon. Where had I heard it before?

I pulled over the notes I had made in Arizona, but his name wasn't there. Then I grabbed the ones I had made the previous afternoon when I looked at the website. Herbert Fallon was the history professor who had graduated the year Heinz would have if he'd lived. I felt elated. They'd known each other as undergraduates.

As I went down the list I found that, except for Professor Fallon, the men on the corridor had scattered across the country. Of the nine undergraduates, two had gone into academic life, both in Illinois. One boy had disappeared. There was no address after his parents' home. Of the six who were left, one was a lawyer in New York City, another a lawyer in Minneapolis. One was unclear, but I had a phone number. Another worked in California. The eighth seemed to have no business connection and no work address, or at least none that he wanted known. And the ninth, of course, was Heinz.

I decided to call the man who had returned to Rimson to teach history first and then the ones on either side of Heinz's room, the one living in Phoenix, his roommate, and the New York lawyer. The Phoenix address had leaped out at me. If the man was living in Phoenix as an undergraduate, he might well have been Heinz's companion on the mountain. No one else on the list lived anywhere near Tucson.

By the time I had finished looking through the material in the package and setting my priorities, it was lunchtime. On the chance that the professor would be in his office, I dialed the college and asked for Herbert Fallon. A moment later a man's voice said, "Fallon."

"Professor Fallon," I began, "my name is Christine Bennett and—"

"Do I know you?" he interrupted sharply.

"No, sir. I'm calling from New York State. I went to high school with someone you knew as an undergraduate at Rimson and I wanted to ask you some questions about him. His name was Heinz Gruner."

"Who?"

"Heinz Gruner. He—"

"Yes, yes, I knew him. We were friends. Who did you say you were?"

I explained again.

"You're looking into his death, is that it?"

"Yes, sir." He sounded so intimidating, I was reduced to sounding like a scared student.

"That's very interesting, very interesting indeed. Heinz Gruner. I must tell you, Miss Bennett, I've been waiting for this call for twenty years."

9

I was hardly able to respond. "I'm so glad to hear it," I said lamely. "I was hoping to find someone who knew him. Do you have time now to discuss some questions about Heinz's death?"

"No, I don't. But I definitely want to talk to you. Give me your number and I'll call you back. Shall we say two hours from now?"

"That will be fine." I gave him my number, made sure he had my name, and hung up. My heart was banging. However our conversation developed, I had hit the jackpot on my first try. I wanted to call Jack and tell him, but I knew his days were very busy and I didn't want to bother him until I had something definitive to say.

Instead, I took my notebook into the kitchen so that I could work while eating, and fixed some egg salad from an egg I had hard-boiled that morning. I added some salad greens and poured a glass of tomato juice. Ordinarily, I eat sandwiches, but Joseph and I had feasted almost every day in Arizona; foregoing the bread for a few weeks could only help the situation.

As I ate, I wrote down questions to ask Professor Fallon. I wanted to know how close their friendship was, what he knew of Heinz's trip to Arizona, who had accompanied him or might have accompanied him. Had Fallon ever met Heinz's parents? The questions filled the page as I ate and wrote. After lunch, I went back to my dining room notes. Perhaps Fallon knew the student whose whereabouts were unknown to the college. Perhaps he knew the man who had no apparent job. Teaching at the college, Fallon would be able to see his classmates every five or ten years when they came to reunions. He might be a gold mine of information. I could hardly believe my good luck.

By the time Fallon called me at a little after two, I was ready for him. "All right," he said, taking the lead, "what has happened that prompted you to call me?"

I went through my story. He interrupted several times, but allowed me to finish. Apparently, his curiosity was stronger than his desire to control the conversation.

"Then it was just a coincidence that you looked into his death, is that right?"

"That's exactly right. I was going to Tucson and I remembered that that was where Heinz had died. The day after my friend and I walked up the trail he took, I met with the Towers, the people who—"

"Not so fast. How did you find this trail? How do you know you went to the right place?"

I told him about Deputy Warren Gonzales.

"I see. And he was the man on the scene when they found Heinz?"

"Yes, he was. And I was able to locate the couple who first spotted the body."

"Who were they?"

"A young married couple at the time." I described our meeting and the crucial new piece of information about the backpack.

85

"Amazing. And no one knew this for twenty years? What kind of police work was that?"

"Professor Fallon, it looked like an accident, a fall off the trail and down a very steep slope. The Towers said only that they had spotted the backpack and the body without mentioning in which direction they were walking. They didn't even realize until we spoke about it that they hadn't seen the backpack on the way up."

"And no one asked. No one thought to ask." He sounded angry and discouraged. "A young man dies and no one considers it anything except an accident."

"Was there any reason that you know of that they should have considered foul play?" I asked, finally inserting a question of my own into the dialogue.

I could hear him exhale a thousand miles away. "No, I suppose there wasn't, at least nothing obvious."

"Then what makes you think they should have considered something other than an accident?"

"Because everyone has a surface life and another life below the surface. When something as huge as a sudden fatality happens, investigators shouldn't go for the neat and obvious and close the books. Heinz was a quiet guy. I liked him. I'm a bully; you can tell that by listening to me. Just verbally; I don't hit people. But I'm another person under the argumentative exterior. Heinz was the opposite. He was this quiet guy who hit the books, listened to classical music, enjoyed his own company. But there was something underneath that was explosive."

"Can you be more specific?" I asked.

86

"He kept most of his life secret. He had a mother and father. I met them when they came out for a parents' weekend once. Quiet, scholarly people. You could see he was their son. But I believe there was more to Heinz's life than those two people and the study of history." He paused. "I think he had friends or acquaintances that no one knew about."

"If no one knew about them, what makes you think they existed?"

"Partly intuition. Partly——" He stopped again.

"Professor Fallon," I said, "if you know something, I would like you to tell me about it. I have reason to believe that Heinz was not alone on that mountain when he fell to his death."

Now the silence was complete. I half expected him to hang up. "Are you there?" I asked.

"I'm here, yes." His voice was subdued, as though the bully had been replaced by the calm inner man. "I saw him once on campus, walking with a man. I only saw them from the rear so I have no idea who his companion was, but I sensed he was older than a student. They were engrossed in whatever their conversation was. I slowed down so I wouldn't catch up with them. I didn't want to disturb them. They reached the library, which is where I was heading myself, and they stopped, shook hands, and the other man walked away, at a much quicker pace. I know this sounds vague and insubstantial—I would never accept such a story from a student trying to prove a point—but we're talking about an event that took place two decades ago and all the parties concerned are dispersed or dead. Had there been an investigation when Heinz died, had someone called me for information, I would have contributed what I knew. The images would have been sharper, the recollections stronger. The first I heard of Heinz's death was when I called him late that summer to find out how the trip was and when he was arriving on campus. His mother answered and broke into tears. I'm not sure she even got my name."

"So you think he had some kind of relationship that he kept secret."

"Let me be clear. I'm not talking about sex, OK? I'm talking about a business relationship, maybe a friendship based on some political or moral affiliation."

"Could it have been drugs?" I asked.

"I doubt it. I never saw Heinz under the influence of anything stronger than music."

I smiled. "You've had twenty years to think about this, Professor. What are your conclusions?"

"I wish I had some. All I have is unanswered questions. But I'm sure there was a part of his life that he kept to himself."

"And that part of his life took him to Arizona?"

"I didn't say that, but it's possible."

"Did you know he was making that trip to Arizona?"

"He talked about it. I knew he was going."

"Was he going alone or with someone?"

"I'm not sure. I think the idea of going was his, and he may have planned originally to go alone. But I don't know how it turned out. Why do you ask?"

"Because there's evidence that he traveled to the

mountain with someone who had a car."

"But that's not the person who reported finding the body."

"No. If someone was with him, he disappeared after the accident. Or whatever it was. And Heinz had no luggage with him."

"Hikers don't carry suitcases. They usually have backpacks."

"The backpack that was found on the trail was too small to carry anything except water and incidentals. There wasn't even a change of socks in it."

"So you think he had a larger backpack somewhere."

"With a toothbrush and some clothes. He could have left it in a hotel room, but then the hotel would have notified his home. But if it was in a car—"

"Then his traveling companion drove away with it."

"Exactly."

"After killing him."

"That's only a possibility," I said. "The companion may have been overcome when he saw Heinz fall to his death and just run away. It wouldn't be the first time someone's courage deserted him at the wrong moment. But yes, whoever this person was, he could have pushed Heinz off the trail at a dangerous place."

"This is all very interesting. I seem to remember that someone on our corridor that year was from Arizona."

I looked down at my notes. "Steven Millman was from Phoenix."

"Steve. That's the guy. I haven't seen him since . . . You know what? I think he dropped out that year."

"Really? You're sure it was that year, the year that Heinz died?"

"I'm positive. There were rumors and gossip that he might have flunked a couple of courses, but I never heard the real story. I'll tell you what. I think I could find his records if you give me a day or two."

"That would be very helpful. What do you remember about him?"

"Smart guy who didn't apply himself. I have a dozen students just like him this semester. If they take the time to study before the final next week, half of them'll pass. The others—good riddance. They've been warned. I'm not a hand-holder. I give them what they need to pass. The rest is up to them."

"Was this Steve Millman on drugs? Alcohol?"

"He drank, but only on weekends. As for drugs, I couldn't tell you. I'm sure he smoked a little hash now and then; everyone did. Did he deal? I don't know."

"I ask because maybe he wanted the contents of Heinz's suitcase. Maybe there was money in there."

"How much money would a kid like that carry? It was probably all in traveler's checks, nice and neat and secure. Did they find his wallet on him?"

"In his pocket. Not much else. I've seen the police file. There was less than a hundred dollars in the wallet and I think he was at the beginning of his trip. He had just finished his exams. The date of his fall was May fifth, Cinco de Mayo in Arizona."

"Ah yes, Cinco de Mayo. So he left right after exams. You're right. He must have had early exams and been at the beginning of his trip. It's even possible his grades were good enough that he was excused from some exams. They used to do that here. They've gotten a little stuffy about that recently."

I was enjoying the professor's candid remarks. "According to the information Dean Hershey sent me, the boy from Phoenix never changed his address."

"I'm glad you talked to Hershey. He's a good guy, a straight shooter. And Heinz and I took a course with him. About Steve Millman, all I can say is I haven't seen him at a reunion. And I get the list."

"I have a question about another person on that corridor. His name is Martin McHugh. Do you remember him?"

"Marty, yeah. He lived next door to me. What about him?"

"There's no information on him after graduation, no address, no work, nothing."

"Interesting. I haven't seen him since we graduated. I don't remember what his major was. I'll ask around."

"That would be helpful. I was planning to call the last number the college has for him, his parents' home. If they're still there, maybe they'll tell me where he is."

"OK. Look, here's what I'm going to do. I have some numbers of friends from my undergraduate days. I'll give them a ring and ask some questions. You want to know about Steve Millman, the guy from Phoenix; Martin McHugh; and anything I can find out about whom Heinz might have gone to Arizona with."

"Yes. I don't know if this case can be resolved, but I'd

like to give it a try. What his mother is most concerned about is whether her son committed suicide."

"Suicide," Fallon said. "He never struck me as depressed or unhappy. He was a quiet guy, but that doesn't mean he was suicidal. And just because I'm loud doesn't mean I'm happy. I'll get back to you, Miss Bennett."

"Chris," I said.

"Chris. I'm Herb, Herb the bully. My wife thinks I'm a pussycat, by the way."

I didn't believe for a moment in the characterization. "I look forward to hearing from you."

I had jotted down several phrases of his as he spoke. He certainly seemed to know the young men on that corridor, and I felt fortunate that I had run into him before I called anyone else. I decided not to call Steve Millman, the student from Phoenix, until Fallon got back to me about why he had dropped out of school. That left six on my list. I dialed the twenty-year-old number for the student who had disappeared, Martin McHugh. It rang and rang. No one answered and no machine picked up, which struck me as odd. Finally I hung up and went on to the next name on my list, the lawyer in New York.

Lawyers know how to insulate themselves. A professional-sounding woman answered with the words, "Law office." I asked for Barry Woodson and she began to interrogate me. I wondered how this man ever acquired new clients. I might well have given up after the first few questions.

"I want to talk to him about something to do with his alma mater, Rimson College," I said.

"Mr. Woodson does not take telephone solicitations."

Gimme a break, I said in my head, echoing my husband—and lately my son. "I am not soliciting. This is an important matter concerning a fellow alumnus of Mr. Woodson."

"Let me see if he's available."

I waited through some clicks, and suddenly a man's voice said, "This is Barry Woodson." He sounded much more friendly than his receptionist, and I began to change my opinion of lawyers.

"Mr. Woodson, my name is Christine Bennett. I went to high school with Heinz Gruner, whom you knew at Rimson College."

"Heinz, yes. My room was next to his one year. Didn't he die in an accident?"

"He did. I'm looking into the events surrounding his fall in Arizona, and some new information about the accident has surfaced."

"How can I help you?"

Whew. I gave him some information, then asked, "Did you happen to accompany him to Arizona on that trip?"

"I've never been to Arizona."

"Do you know whether Heinz made the trip alone or went with a friend?"

"You know, I hardly remember talking about it. I think he wanted to hike somewhere and then during the summer I heard, maybe from a friend, that he'd had an accident and died. When I got back to campus in the fall, no one seemed to know much about what happened."

"The accident took place on a mountain north of Tucson. Someone on your dormitory corridor that year was from Phoenix. His name was Steve Millman. Do you remember him?"

"Steve, yes, I do remember him. I think he dropped out of school."

"He did. Do you know if he went to Arizona with Heinz?"

"Miss Bennett, you're asking me to recall a small detail of my college life that must have taken place close to twenty years ago. I hardly remember that Heinz was planning a trip to Arizona. I have no idea whether Steve or anyone else had plans to go with him."

"Were you friendly with Steve?"

"We had a class together now and then. It's a small school so we all got to know each other. I knew him but I wouldn't characterize our relationship as being friends. And I never saw him after that year."

"Was there anyone on that corridor who was your friend?"

"Herb Fallon. We were buddies. He's on the faculty now: History Department. He comes to New York once in a while and we get together. You should give him a call."

"I've already spoken to him. I'd like to ask you about one other student. His name is Martin McHugh."

"Marty, yes. I knew him."

"The college has only his telephone number from the time he was a student, and they've never heard from him. Have you, by any chance?"

"Sorry. We graduated and I never saw him again."

"Thank you, Mr. Woodson. May I call you again if I have some more specific questions?"

"Sure. If something happened to Heinz that wasn't an accident, I'd like to know about it."

I thanked him and ended the call.

Now I would wait to hear from Herbert Fallon. I had done enough for one day and had plenty of leads to follow.

10

I had not yet told Jack about my day when the phone rang after dinner and Professor Fallon announced himself.

"Yes," I said, feeling as eager as I'm sure I sounded. "Do you have something for me?"

"I got over to the records office before they closed this afternoon. This fellow Steven Millman from Phoenix is an interesting story. There's a note in his file that he failed to arrive for the fall semester, and his family called and then wrote to ask for their tuition and other expenses back."

"Sounds like he made a last-minute decision. I assume they would have had to send a check for the fall term some weeks in advance."

"Definitely. So whatever changed his mind occurred

late in the summer, months after Heinz's death. About a year after that, Steve wrote to the registrar to see if he could reapply for admission. They said he could but he never took the step. That's the last correspondence of record."

"And there's no explanation of why he failed to show up that fall?"

"Nothing. His parents simply wrote that he decided to drop out of school and pursue other endeavors—those are the words they used—and they hoped this would not prejudice his possible readmission at a later time. It's a carefully worded letter. I almost have the feeling a lawyer helped them write it. I called the last phone number for the Millmans, but it's been changed."

"I'll see what I can do to find him," I said.

"I also looked into the fellow who graduated and was never heard from again, Martin McHugh. There's nothing in the records that would indicate a problem with the college, so I called an old friend who knew him. He said Marty just didn't relate to reunions and sports, and since he didn't love Rimson, he's never written a check."

"Did your friend have a phone number for McHugh?"

"Got it right here." He read off a number with a familiar area code.

"He's in New York?" I said.

"Lives and works there. I think he's in broadcasting or television or some such."

"I'll call him tomorrow. Looks like we're doing

pretty well here." I told him I had spoken to Barry Woodson.

"Barry, right. He practices law."

"Yes, and he thought you might be able to help me."

"We're in touch from time to time. Well, that's all I've got for you tonight. I'll make some more phone calls and let you know what I find out."

The whereabouts of Martin McHugh had turned out to be simple and straightforward, not a hint of mystery about it. He had graduated and put his college days behind him.

Jack had been making coffee as I spoke to Herbert Fallon, and I could smell it when I got off the phone. We sat in our usual places in the family room, the file between us. I opened it and showed him the sketch of the dorm corridor and all the information I had received that morning from Dean Hershey.

"The guy sounds very cooperative," Jack said. "This is nice. And he got it to you fast."

"He knew Heinz and he wants to know what happened on that mountain."

"Who just called?"

I explained and then told him what I'd learned during the day about the young men on that corridor twenty years ago. "And my big mystery isn't a mystery anymore. He's alive and well and living in New York. He just doesn't send checks to Rimson."

"Not everyone does. In big universities, only a small percentage of graduates ever contribute. They make their money from the handful of financially successful

97

alumni who have a conscience—or want to be remembered as big givers. Sounds like you've had a busy day."

"Very busy. You were lucky to get fed tonight. It's just that I got hungry myself."

"Glad to hear it. So you've got a guy on that corridor who lived in Phoenix and never came back to Rimson after Heinz's accident. Sounds promising."

"Except I don't know where he is. Herb Fallon is going to try to locate him. I've been lucky so far, finding a dean who knew Heinz and then this Professor Fallon. He's quite a character: refers to himself as a bully—which he sounds like—and says his wife thinks he's a pussycat."

Jack gave me the grin. "It's the only way she can stay married to him. You probably think I'm a pushover, too."

"Well. Only sometimes." I told him about Herb Fallon's description of Heinz and the mysterious stranger.

"That's pretty thin. Even if Fallon is convinced the stranger wasn't a student or professor at Rimson, that doesn't exclude the community outside the college. The guy could have been from a church or a local radio station or someplace in town where Gruner was trying to get a part-time job. Fallon made it seem sub rosa, but more likely it was just a meeting of two people who had something to say to each other."

"I'll see where it fits when I learn more," I said noncommittally. Jack often pooh-poohs some of my unusual findings, but in his own work he treats such information more seriously.

"What I think you're on to is the lack of a change of clothes and transportation to the mountain. Somebody drove Gruner there and then disappeared, probably with another backpack or suitcase. Doesn't mean he did anything to Gruner. He may have panicked when Gruner fell down the mountain and just took off. But this missing man is the key to what happened."

"I hope Herb Fallon gets back to me with the Phoenix guy's address and phone number. In the meantime, I'll call Martin McHugh in the morning, the one I thought was missing for twenty years but seems to be alive and working in New York."

"Home of missing persons."

"I wonder if the other man could have been Herb Fallon."

Jack laughed. "Now you're starting to sound like your jaded, suspicious husband."

"Wish I were as good a cook."

"It'll come," Jack said. "We're not married ten years yet."

I lingered over the *Times* with my last cup of coffee after Jack and Eddie were gone on Wednesday morning. Then I sat back, the cup empty, the world news folded to the editorial page. As I sat thinking, not of the news but of the Heinz Gruner case, I realized I had all but given up the idea that Heinz had committed suicide. It wasn't completely out of the question. He might have jumped off the path without warning, even with a friend standing nearby, helpless to stop him. But I didn't think so. And in making that decision, I had accomplished all that Mrs. Gruner wanted, the knowledge that her son's death had been something other than suicide. I was sure that murder had never entered her mind, but it had certainly entered mine. And I would not disregard the mysterious stranger. Now that I knew about him, I could ask the other former students if they had knowledge of this person.

I cleaned up the kitchen, wiping up my son's crumbs, and opened my notebook to the page with Martin McHugh's phone number. I never call people at the very beginning of the business day. I give them a chance to be late, to grab a cup of coffee, to talk to fellow workers, and finally to sit at their desk to start their day. Mr. McHugh had another ten minutes coming.

The phone rang about eight minutes later.

"Herb Fallon here."

"Good morning."

"I had a busy night after we talked. I've been trying to find Steven Millman, our friend from Phoenix who left Rimson and never came back."

"Yes," I said, hoping I didn't sound too eager.

"I talked to his mother last night."

"Really? Is she still in Phoenix?"

"Yes, she is, still in the same house but with a new number."

"Did she give you a number for Steve?"

100

"Not only did she *not* give me a number, she acted pretty cagey when I asked her for it. I tried to make like I was an old friend who'd lost touch, but she wouldn't budge. Finally she asked for my number and said she'd see if she could find him—those were her words—and if she did, she'd let him know I was trying to reach him. It doesn't sound too promising. If he's told her not to give out his number, or if she really doesn't know where her son is, I think we have a problem."

"Interesting," I said. "I wonder if he's changed his name."

"That's a pretty big step."

"Not if you're trying to disappear. And it certainly looks as though that's what he's done."

Fallon muttered a few words of agreement. Then he said, "Have you talked to McHugh yet?"

"I was just about to call when the phone rang."

"McHugh might know where Millman is. I think they were friends. The truth is, most of us on that corridor that year were at least friendly toward each other. Some of us became lifelong friends; others just remained good acquaintances. I'd like to know what happened to Millman."

"Maybe his mother will call you back."

"And maybe one of us'll find out where he is through another channel. Let me know how your conversation with Marty McHugh goes."

"I will. And thanks for calling."

I decided to ask Jack later to see if Steven Millman's name came up on his computer as a felon or having been arrested. I suspected it wouldn't, but Jack might know where to look to eke out some tidbit of information. Why does a young man of nineteen or twenty drop out of school, fiddle with the possibility of coming back, and then drop out of life? I could hardly imagine Jack's mother telling a college buddy of his that she would see if she could find him. If Steve Millman had not completed college, it might limit his future achievements. Perhaps he had finished elsewhere under his name and then dropped out of sight. But most of all, the coincidence of his not returning to Rimson after Heinz's death raised a red flag.

I set aside my discomfort and dialed the number Fallon had given me for Martin McHugh. It rang several times. Then a mechanical voice came on to tell me that—and here McHugh inserted his own name in his own voice—was unavailable and please leave a name and number. I declined to do so. There were other options, one of them being a chat with an operator. Maybe later, I thought. I didn't want to give up too much myself and give him the upper hand. Perhaps he refused to answer his phone at all until the caller was identified.

I pulled out the sketch of the dorm corridor. I had already spoken to or attempted to contact four of the students: Fallon, Millman, McHugh, and Woodson. Heinz was the fifth person, leaving four more names on the list. I had not picked the original four at random. Either their rooms were close to Heinz's or they had some attribute, like living in Phoenix, that prompted me to start there. Now it was time to assess the last four.

A man named Andrew Franklin lived and worked in Minneapolis. There was a time difference, but it was late enough in the morning that he would be at work. A pleasant woman answered, noting the name of a law firm, and I asked to speak to Mr. Franklin. She was much easier to deal with than Barry Woodson's receptionist in New York, and in a few moments I was talking to Mr. Franklin.

"Heinz Gruner," he said. "I haven't heard that name mentioned in many years. I knew him, of course. We were both students at Rimson, but he suffered a fatal accident."

"That's what I'm calling about," I said, having been given my opening. I reminded him about the accident and told him I had known Heinz in high school. "I'm trying to learn exactly what led to his accident, and Dean Hershey gave me a list of all the students who lived on Heinz's corridor that semester."

"What's your theory?"

"I think someone was with him on that mountain, Mr. Franklin. Did you travel to Arizona that spring?"

"Never set foot in the state. I thrive on cold weather."

I was happy to hear someone did. "Do you know who accompanied him or who might have met him down there?"

"Not an inkling. I remember the morning he took off from school. I helped him down to a taxi with his luggage. He was trying to do it all by himself and I figured

103

he'd topple down the stairs if he didn't have help."

I perked up. "You helped him with his luggage?"

"Down to the taxi, yes."

"Do you remember how much he had?"

"Couple of heavy suitcases. That was before the day of these wheelie things. You had to hoist those old ones and boy, were his old. Looked like they came from the Old World."

They probably had, I thought. "Do you recall if he had a backpack, Mr. Franklin?"

"I'm sure he didn't."

"Was he going to Arizona directly from school?"

"Oh yes. He had finished the one or two finals he had to take and was on his way. I was in the dorm that morning studying for one of my own or I wouldn't have been around to help. He was flying to Phoenix."

"His luggage was never recovered after the accident," I said. "That's why I'm asking."

"Hard to misplace that big one of his. I could hardly lift it. Must have had all his clothes from the whole year. Maybe he was planning on buying a backpack when he got to Phoenix. I know he intended to do some climbing. He told me as we jockeyed those bags down the stairs."

"Did he say with whom?"

"If he did, it didn't register."

"Do you remember a student named Steven Millman?"

"Steve? Sure. He was on the same corridor that year."

"He lived in Phoenix," I said. "You don't happen to

remember if he was in the same taxi intending to join Heinz in Arizona?"

"No idea. Wait a minute. There was something strange about Millman. Let me think." A few silent seconds passed. "He dropped out of school."

"That's what I heard."

"You know, I never connected his dropping out with Heinz's death until this minute." He sounded distressed.

"I don't know if there is a connection," I said, "but it's one of the things I'm working on."

"Interesting. Have you spoken to Millman?"

I told him what had happened when Herb Fallon called Millman's mother.

"So he's made himself unavailable. You know, I never heard about Heinz's accident till I got back to campus that fall. We had a convocation the first day we were back and the dean told us. I didn't know Steve was gone until a couple of weeks into the semester when it just came to me that he wasn't there."

"Was anyone in your class a close friend of Steve?"

"I don't know. I think he had a double room that last year. His roommate was—"

"Arthur Howell?" I asked, reading the name off my diagram.

"Artie, right. Give Artie a call. He'll know where Steve is."

I wasn't as convinced as Mr. Franklin, but I was certainly going to try. "I will do that. Just to get my notes

105

right: no one else was taking Heinz's taxi to the airport, correct?"

"Correct. When the suitcases were in the trunk, the driver took off. There were two heavy suitcases and no backpack."

"You've been very helpful, Mr. Franklin." I finished off the conversation with my usual request that he get in touch if he remembered anything new. He promised he would, and I thought he sounded sincere. After twenty years of not giving Heinz Gruner and his death a thought, Andrew Franklin had suddenly had his eyes opened to possibilities he had never dreamed of.

For my part, I now knew that Heinz had taken off with heavy luggage. What had become of it?

11

The person to talk to was Mrs. Gruner. There was a possibility that Heinz had shipped one or both suitcases back home before he got on his flight to Phoenix. That was something she would remember. And if she never saw any of his luggage again, even in her grief she would likely recall that fact.

I got in my car and drove over to Hillside Village. It wasn't quite lunchtime yet, and I was able to catch her sitting in a sunny room enclosed in glass at the back of the building. She was talking to a woman about her age, but when she saw me she brightened and waved me over. The other woman got up and walked away, joining a small group near the window.

We caught up for a few minutes like old friends. I told her she looked better than when I'd last seen her, and she admitted that she'd decided to become more active, to spend less time in her room and more time among the residents.

"I think it's doing you good," I said. "I want to tell you what I've been doing since I last saw you." I told her about my trip to Arizona, leading in gently to my visit to Picacho Peak Park.

"You went there?" She seemed astounded.

"It's a beautiful place," I said. "And I wanted to see if I could learn more about Heinz's death."

Her face became sober, the lines in her forehead deeper. "You found out something, Chris?"

"I found out a few things and I have some questions for you."

"I will tell you anything I know."

The first thing I did was go over the names of the young men on the dormitory corridor. I read them off slowly, asking her if any of them sounded familiar. She listened attentively as I read each one, then shook her head, appearing discouraged. When I said, "Herb Fallon," though, she perked up.

"Herb," she repeated. "Herbie. Maybe he knew a Herbie. Maybe I heard that name from him."

"He's a professor at Rimson now," I said. "He liked Heinz very much."

"A professor," she said sadly. "My boy would have been a professor."

I waited. Finally, she told me to continue. I read off

the last few names. One sounded somewhat familiar, but she could identify no one as good friend or best friend or hiking companion. The name Steve Millman rang no bell.

"I want to ask you about Heinz's luggage," I said.

"What luggage?"

"He took suitcases to school, didn't he?"

"In the fall, yes. In the spring he brought them home."

"But that spring he flew to Phoenix."

"So what happened to his luggage?" she asked.

"That's my question."

She thought quietly. "If my husband were here, he would remember. Wait, wait. Yes, something happened with the suitcases. There were two. One we had from Germany. The other we bought when he started at Rimson. When he came home for holidays, he brought the smaller one with him. But he went from Rimson to Arizona that spring; I remember that. He took all of it with him. When he died and my husband went out, there was no suitcase, just a—what do you call it? One of those things you carry on your back when you hike."

"A backpack," I said.

"A small backpack. No clothes."

"Did your husband inquire after the suitcases?"

She shrugged. "Maybe. It was the least of our problems." She closed her eyes. "There was something," she said, "something funny about the suitcases. Let me think a moment."

I stood and walked to the large window. Beautiful plantings and a small waterfall were just beyond the glass, separated by a path for walkers. I was impressed with the care this institution had taken for the sake of beauty. At this time of year, the greenery was lush and the water so clear it made me thirsty.

"Chris."

I turned. Mrs. Gruner's eyes were open, wide open.

"A suitcase came to the house. I remember now. It was after my husband came back, after the funeral. The doorbell rang one morning and when I opened the door, there was a man with a piece of paper for me to sign. I was so shocked when I saw the suitcase, I could hardly breathe. It was as though Heinz were about to walk through the open door. Only there was no Heinz. There was just a suitcase."

"Who sent it?"

"I don't know. It was paid for, I remember that. I asked the man if I had to pay and he said no, it was all taken care of. I called my husband and told him. I wouldn't open it till he came home."

"Was it locked?" I asked.

"Not with a key. With some wire. If you opened the wire, it broke."

"For security," I said. "Did you have the key?"

"It was on the key ring in Heinz's pocket. He had the key to our house and the keys for both suitcases. But only one suitcase came, and we never found out who sent it."

"Do you remember what was in it?"

"Clothes. Clean clothes, dirty clothes. Some school-books. There was nothing important, nothing that could tell us what had happened to our son on that mountain."

"What did you do with the suitcase?"

"I don't remember anymore. I washed the clothes, I hung them up in his closet. Later on, after my husband died, after I had my stroke and I knew I couldn't live there by myself, I gave away everything that I couldn't take with me to Hillside Village."

I thought how terrible that must have been, disposing of the clothing and mementos of the two people she had loved most. I, too, had a husband and a son—a husband who had achieved a great deal because of his hard work and strong commitment, and a son who we hoped would go even further with his life.

"Did you try to find out who had sent the suitcase?" I asked.

"My husband called the police. They said there was no suitcase. They had given him everything they had."

"Which was the wallet, the keys, and the small back-pack."

"Yes. That was all. And we never got the second suit-case."

"Do you know what was missing from his things?"

"No. He had simple clothes, enough to go a week before doing a laundry. If a blue shirt was missing or a pair of jeans they were all wearing, how should I know? And why should I care? Nothing mattered to me any-more."

"I understand. Tell me, did you speak to him often on the phone?"

"Not so often. We wrote letters."

"Letters," I said with surprise. In the years I had taught English at St. Stephen's, I had come to realize that correspondence between students and parents was rare. The telephone provided the main, if not the only, link between the generations. Checks came in the mail and little else. Today even that has probably changed, and e-mail has replaced the phone.

"My husband used to get angry at big phone bills. He said it was cheaper and more permanent to write letters."

"Your husband was right," I said. "Do you have Heinz's letters?"

"I have every letter he ever wrote to me."

At that moment, a bell sounded. People rose and started toward the dining hall.

"Would you mind if I read the letters he wrote you his last year at Rimson?"

"I can find them for you. I don't have to go to lunch. We can—"

I smiled. "Yes, you do have to go to lunch, Mrs. Gruner. I'll walk you over. I'll come back this afternoon."

She began to argue, but I assured her there was no hurry. We walked together, and at the door to the dining room we said good-bye.

Letters, I thought as I walked out to the car. Pieces of paper with writing on them. I began to giggle. Who could have imagined a cache of letters that might answer all sorts of questions about Heinz Gruner's life?

I went home and made myself a healthy salad, ate it

with gusto, and read my paper. When Jack called, just to say hello, I told him the news.

"He wrote *letters?*" my disbelieving husband said. "I thought those went out with the cavemen."

"You never know, do you? Anyway, we know for sure that Heinz left Rimson with two suitcases, and someone went through them, took what he wanted, and returned the rest. Someone was with him, Jack. Someone joined him on the flight or met him in Phoenix."

"How many detectives you got working on this with you?"

I laughed. "Just the usual. Hey, if you've got some spare time, see what you can find out about a guy named Steven Millman." I gave him all the information I had.

"Sure, I'll do that little favor for you, honey. I'm expecting to have some spare time next January. That suit your investigation?"

"OK, Lieutenant. I'll back off."

"If we could just get rid of those civilians, we'd have a pretty nice life here. I'll see what I can do." He read back what I had told him and I approved it. "You going to read those letters?"

"I'm going to try to do it this afternoon. Eddie's taken care of after school, so I have a couple of empty hours. I'll start with the last ones and work backward. Maybe he mentions a name that's not on my list."

"Have fun. I've gotta run."

I waited an hour, in case Mrs. Gruner wanted to take a nap after lunch. Then I drove back to Hillside Village.

Many residents were sitting in the sun. At one table, four women were playing cards. A man and a woman were playing chess at another. Mrs. Gruner was not in the group.

I went inside and the receptionist called upstairs. "She's waiting for you. Can you find your way?"

"Sure."

The door to Mrs. Gruner's room was ajar. I tapped on it and pushed it open. Mrs. Gruner was sitting on the bed, a carton beside her.

"Come in, come in," she said. "I have all the letters right here. These," she lifted a stack tied with a ribbon, "are from my husband. He wrote to me when we first knew each other."

"Did you live far apart?" I asked.

"No. We lived quite close, but he liked to write letters. He was an old-fashioned man, but a good one. And he wrote beautiful letters."

I looked at the top envelope. It was addressed in black ink in nearly illegible handwriting. An unusual stamp was stuck in the upper right-hand corner, and I realized this correspondence had taken place in Germany.

"The rest are from my son." That was most of the letters in the carton. They were sorted into packets about four to six inches thick. "These are the ones from his last year at Rimson." She handed me one. The top letter had a postmark of May second, the last letter Heinz had written his parents before taking off for Arizona.

I took the pack and sat in a chair. "May I sit and read?"

"Of course. I will leave you alone for a while, Chris. We can talk when I come back."

I started to protest, but she was already on the phone, asking for assistance to go downstairs. When the aide came, she left with him. I waited a few minutes, then untied the string and set the letters down on an end table with the last letter on top. It was an eerie feeling.

The top of the envelope, like all the other envelopes in the collection, had been sliced open cleanly. I reached in and pulled out the single sheet of paper. It was dated and began, "Dear Mom and Dad." He described the take-home final in German literature he had completed and just turned in. He thought he had done pretty well on that. He was finished now and beginning to pack for his trip. He thanked them for the gift of this vacation he was so looking forward to.

He would be the first to leave the dorm the next morning. Right now it was very quiet, everyone studying. He talked about some courses, mentioned a professor who had excused him from a final, said that one of the boys on the corridor had fallen asleep the night before while studying and didn't wake up till breakfast time, almost hysterical at the hours he had lost. There was no mention of a traveling companion to Arizona or a specific destination.

At the end of the letter, which continued to the second side of the sheet, he finished with a few lines in German. I know a little French, but not a word of German. It seemed that the lines were personal, affectionate comments to his parents, having nothing to do with school. I put the letter away and started on the second.

In this one he mentioned going out to dinner with Herbie and Barry—the lawyer I had spoken to the day before, most likely—and described the hamburger he had eaten, obviously one of his own design. I sensed the fun of being at a college far from home, the freedom students had, the pleasure of dropping petty responsibilities like eating at prescribed times or keeping one's room clean, instead being able to associate with this one for a meal and that one for a good discussion. Nowhere did I sense sadness or heartache. This was a young man reaching the end of another year at a fine college, putting his finals behind him, looking forward to a trip.

I worked my way backward in time, from envelope to envelope. Professors were mentioned. Herbie had decided on a major in American history. Heinz had decided definitely on European history. He would apply for a Fulbright to Germany in his senior year. Professor Hershey was all for it.

But although the letters were well written and newsy, they didn't add to my knowledge of the Arizona trip. He mentioned when the airline tickets arrived and said he would buy a backpack when he got there. It would be easier that way. I raced through the envelopes, wanting to read as much as I could before Mrs. Gruner returned. I was already back in the winter of that year, reading descriptions of deep snow, narrow paths plowed between buildings, when I came to a sentence that stopped me: "I saw K on campus today. He's fine and sends his regards." And on to an anecdote about someone answering the wrong question in class that morning.

K, I thought. Someone who isn't often on campus. Maybe I had found the mysterious stranger.

12

Mrs. Gruner returned shortly afterward. She stepped carefully off the wheelchair and walked unaided into the room, turning to thank the man who had pushed her to her door.

"It's a beautiful day," she said, lowering herself into the second chair in the room. "Have you had time to read some letters?"

I told her she was lucky to have them, that Heinz was a fine letter writer, and I had learned much about the people at Rimson and how the college worked. She accepted my comments with her usual mixture of pleasure and sadness.

"He doesn't write much about the trip," I said.

"No. He would tell us afterward how it was. He had his ticket, he had some pocket money."

"How did he pick Arizona?" I asked.

"He heard about it. He read about it."

"Maybe someone he knew at school lived there?"

She considered that. "Yes, maybe."

"But you think he went alone."

"I don't know. We sent him one plane ticket. If he

went with a friend, then his friend would get his own ticket."

"Of course." I pulled out the winter letter with the reference to K and read her the two brief sentences. "Do you remember who this person was?"

I am sure her face changed. She was a plain woman with pale skin, probably because she didn't spend much time outside. I can't say she ever looked happy; at best, she looked neutral. But when I read those sentences aloud, something fearful flickered over her face.

"What was the name?" she asked, her voice unsteady.

"There is no name, just the letter K, as in Kafka," I said, making a small joke.

"I don't know anyone named Kafka. When is this letter? When did he write it?"

I looked at the date. "In March. It was still winter."

"What does this have to do with Arizona?" There was anger in her voice, or at the very least annoyance.

"I don't know what it has to do with Arizona. I'm trying to find out if someone was with Heinz when he had his hiking accident."

"Well, surely this, this K would not have been with him."

"Why are you so sure?" The change in her demeanor was so striking, I felt it was necessary to press forward.

"Because—because he has no name. He is not one of the friends. He is not a professor. He is nobody."

"Mrs. Gruner, your son wrote to you that he saw someone that you and your husband knew by name.

117

This man sent you regards. If you prefer not to talk about him—"

"I'm tired. This has been a difficult day, going through the letters, talking about all this again. I need my *Mittags schläfchen*."

"Excuse me?"

"My nap, my afternoon nap. If you will excuse me."

I stuck the letter back in its envelope, tied the group together with the original string, wished her a good sleep, and went home.

"Well, that's crazy," Melanie Gross said when I finished the story. Her kids were in one place, my son in another, and we had a rare childless late afternoon together.

"Could I have hurt her feelings in some way when I said 'Kafka'?" I asked.

"Ridiculous. Kafka's a famous writer. Whoever this K person is, he's roused some old memory that she doesn't want to confront. Or that she doesn't want you privy to. Something secret in her life."

"Or Heinz's life."

"Where is Rimson located?" Mel asked.

"In the middle of nowhere in Illinois. Some guy named Theodore Rimson had a large piece of property that he gave to a group of men who were trying to start a liberal arts college about a hundred years ago."

"For men."

"Of course for men. How many people thought women could fill a college back then? According to the literature the dean sent me, it became coed in the 1920s, long before Harvard, Yale, and Princeton decided to do the same thing."

"So it's in the middle of nowhere, which means that if Mr. K wanted to have a talk with Heinz Gruner, either he lived near the college or he made a special trip there to see him."

"Exactly."

"So it wasn't a case of Heinz walking down a path and seeing Mr. K and saying, 'Hi there, how are you?'"

"It was by appointment."

"No one on your list has a name starting with K?"

I shook my head. "Mel, K could be Karl. K could be Kenneth or Kevin or Keith."

"He could be professor emeritus, maybe someone who knew Heinz's parents."

"Then what's she so upset for? You should have seen the transformation in her personality when I read her those two sentences saying Heinz had seen K on campus, that he was fine and sent his regards."

"She's holding something back. Just the fact that her son referred to him as K instead of by name shows there's something secret about him."

"You're right. Funny, Herb Fallon mentioned what was probably this meeting between Heinz and someone not from the college. They didn't meet secretly, but Heinz handled the meeting as though it was a secret from everyone except his parents."

"Which means the man had nothing to do with the

college," Mel said. "He traveled to the college to see Heinz."

"Who would do that?" I said, almost to myself. "I don't even have an idea of how old this man is, but I assume older than an undergraduate. He knows the elder Gruners. He's on good terms with them because he sends them regards. He has some special connection to Heinz."

"He's Heinz's real father," Mel said.

"You do come up with startling possibilities."

"He's a wealthy friend of the family who paid for Heinz's education as long as Heinz made a B average."

"I don't think B would cut it in that family."

"Then A-minus. And he checked on Heinz every year, maybe every semester."

"That could be, Mel. I don't think the Gruners were wealthy people. I'm sure Rimson was always expensive, although they probably give scholarships to good students."

"Maybe K was just an old friend who was interviewing for a faculty job and looked up your friend Heinz to say hello."

"Then what's all the secrecy about? Mrs. Gruner practically threw me out of her room over this person. She won't talk about him. She doesn't even want to think about him."

"You've got yourself a problem, Chris. I've given you three wonderful scenarios. I don't think I have the energy to come up with a fourth."

I smiled and Mel laughed. It was late afternoon, and she had taught all day. She was doing pretty well in the energy department from what I could see.

"I'll have to keep at this," I said. "But I'm afraid my friendship with Mrs. Gruner has ended. I don't know how to handle this."

"Give her a few days and call her up, just to see how she is. Offer her a drive. Take her to lunch. You're certainly a gracious person. She'll thaw. Maybe she'd like to visit your house. Can you imagine what it's like to live in Hillside Village for years and never see the inside of a house?"

I had already done that. "I just hope she agrees to talk to me."

I walked home slowly, admiring the flowering trees on both sides of the street that made spring so beautiful in the Northeast. Shiny new leaves were appearing daily on shrubs and deciduous trees. Spring is really my season.

I still had half an hour before Eddie would be dropped off, and dinner required only warming up. I fished out the phone number for Martin McHugh and dialed it, preparing to disconnect before the voice mail picked up.

"Yeah, McHugh," a harried voice said.

"Mr. McHugh, my name is Chris Bennett and I was a friend of a Rimson classmate of yours."

"Rimson. That's awhile." The voice a little less harried.

"Heinz Gruner. Do you remember him?"

"Lived on my corridor one year. I'm sorry to tell you he died, if you don't already know."

"I do know. It's why I'm calling you."

"Where are you, Miss—"

"Chris Bennett. I'm calling from Oakwood, New York."

"Oakwood, yeah. I have friends up that way. I'm in the middle of something right now. Would it be possible for me to call you later on?"

"Sure." I gave him my number.

"Better than that. Could I take you to lunch tomorrow? I'd like to get away from the office for a while anyway and I have a club nearby. How's twelve fifteen?"

Considering that McHugh had been on my "lost" list, this was quite a turn of events. "That would be lovely. Just tell me where."

He gave me directions, told me where to park, and we had a lunch date. I hung up grinning, with twenty minutes before Eddie came home. I dialed Herb Fallon's number.

He was there and curious about my conversation with Martin McHugh. "Lunch at a club," he said. "I knew I was in the wrong profession."

"There's more, Herb. I found something in one of Heinz's letters that I think ties in with your seeing him with a mysterious stranger." I recited the two lines from memory.

"Letters?" he said. "You found his letters?"

I explained.

"You're really going great guns, Chris. I'll bet that's the guy I saw him with. It was winter, as I remember. I don't know anyone at Rimson with a K."

"I've been calling him Mr. Kafka."

"From the sound of it, you'll have as much trouble finding out who he was as the poor guy in Kafka's book."

I told him about Mrs. Gruner's reaction.

"Very interesting. She knows about him and wants to keep him a secret. Looks like you've stumbled on something important."

"But I don't know where to go with it. Could this man have been a professor emeritus?"

"I'll look at the records but I'm not optimistic."

"Were there any organizations at Rimson that might have invited an outside speaker?" It had just occurred to me that speakers popped up on college campuses all the time.

"Yes, there are. You may have hit on something. What's today? Wednesday," he said, answering his own question. "I have some free time tomorrow morning. Let me see if I can scrape up some old information. We have frequent speakers, as well as musical performers, sometimes a dance troupe. Your Mr. K could have been any of those. Good thinking. I'll call you when I've finished my digging."

I reminded him I was going into the city to have lunch with Martin McHugh, so I might not be back before three. He asked me to save him a menu.

123

· · ·

"That's a pretty fancy place to have lunch," Jack said when I told him.

"Which makes me nervous, as I'm sure you can understand. I suppose I should wear my black suit and look like a New York woman taking time from her busy day at the office to entertain a client."

Jack thought that was pretty funny. "Good thing you have a black suit. They might not let you in."

"Stop scaring me. Want to hear Mel's scenarios for who this Mr. K might be?"

"I'm listening."

I went through them, making him laugh louder at each suggestion. I had actually taken them quite seriously. Mrs. Gruner's reaction to my discovery of those two lines in Heinz's letter had been so unexpected and irrational that I was willing to believe almost anything about Mr. K.

"Well, she's got a good imagination. Maybe this McHugh guy will clue you in on something more substantial. I like your idea, by the way, that K was a speaker or a musician. It fits with the school."

"And it's not a stretch to imagine that K knew the Gruners."

"Well, the way you're going, you'll probably have it all worked out by the weekend."

13

Martin McHugh had given me two parking garage options: one right near the club, the other about two blocks away. Needless to say, the farther one was less expensive, and that's the one I headed toward. I had allotted my time well and arrived inside the club building six minutes before our meeting time. I smoothed my hair, which is most of what I do to make myself look presentable, then glanced at the handful of people standing around the lobby, obviously waiting, as I was, to meet someone.

From where I stood, I could see down the inside half-dozen stairs to the outer doors. A man pushed a door, clambered up the stairs, and pushed open an inner door near where I stood. He stopped and surveyed the lobby area, turning slowly, finally fixing his eyes on me. "Miss Bennett?"

"Mr. McHugh?"

He held out his hand. "Glad to meet you. Let's go upstairs."

The club was on the top floor. We took an express elevator, paused at the receptionist's desk only long enough for Mr. McHugh to wave and smile, then walked inside the dining area. We were shown to a table near a window with a view of the Empire State Building. I had never before had the sensation of sitting on top of the world.

"I always get the buffet," he said as the menus were

handed to us. "But you're welcome to order off the menu. I like variety. What about you?"

"I like it, too. I'll join you."

"Let's go."

We walked to a smaller, viewless room and filled our plates with delicous-looking salads. The hot dishes, which we would come back for, sounded wonderful. I was sorry the invitation hadn't included Jack, who has the better palate and the greater capacity.

Back at our table, Martin McHugh said, "So what's the story you're looking for?"

I gave him a briefing.

"That was a nice year," he said nostalgically. "A good crowd on the corridor. No obvious crackpots or shirkers. I can't tell you I was Heinz's best friend because I wasn't, but he was a good guy: quiet, studious, a nice person to have around. When I heard about the accident, it threw me for a loop."

"Before we talk about that, I wonder if you'd mind telling me why you've never had anything to do with Rimson since you graduated. Most of the other men who lived on that corridor have kept in touch with the college, gone back for reunions, updated their addresses. You didn't."

"There was a reason. Your question brings back the other part of the Rimson experience, the negative. Happened my senior year. I was all set to graduate, had a good record, one or two misses but nothing terrible, when an English teacher called me in and accused me of plagiarizing a paper I had written. I assume you know how serious a charge that is."

"I do."

"He said another student's paper had almost identical language in some parts, had the same factual error that I made somewhere, and it was clear I had copied from him."

"Or he from you."

"He didn't put it that way, but yes, you're right. That was the other alternative. I was told I wouldn't graduate."

"How terrible," I said spontaneously. "What did you do?"

"I worked hard not to go to pieces. The professor wouldn't even entertain the possibility that the other guy stole from me, which is what I was sure had happened. Either that or the most unlikely coincidence in the history of the college had occurred. Bottom line, I didn't graduate. We were a less litigious society at that time and my parents, who believed me, didn't hire a lawyer and make threats. We just talked to a dean, who resolved the problem by allowing me to take another English course elsewhere. When I finished it—with an A, by the way—they sent me my diploma."

"What an ordeal," I said. "And to have such a weight hanging over you all these years."

"Well, there's a silver lining, if you can call it that. Several years ago at a conference, I ran into the guy I was supposed to have cribbed from. I cornered him and got him to confess that he'd read the draft of my paper while I was out of my room. I had a tape recorder in my pocket to tape some of the speakers, and I was smart enough to record the conversation, although the quality was pretty awful. I sent it to the English professor, who agreed to reinstate my grade for that semester. Nothing was ever done to the son of a bitch who actually plagiarized."

"Or to the professor, I bet."

"He still thinks he's God." McHugh buttered a roll and took a bite. A waiter came and dropped off our wine. "Well, here's to solving mysteries." McHugh touched his glass to mine. "So now you know why I don't write checks to my alma mater. I'll tell you, if anyone ever did that to my son, I'd put the college out of business."

I could believe it from the passion in his voice. "I'm glad you were tough enough to survive."

"But you didn't come here to talk about my problems. What's up with Heinz Gruner?"

I told him.

"So you're looking for information on that trip he took to Arizona."

"And anyone who might have gone with him or met him there."

"Well, it wasn't me. I've never been to Arizona. Took a vacation in Florida last year and I go to California frequently, but never Arizona."

"Do you remember any discussion about his trip?"

"I couldn't have dredged it up without your background stuff, but now that I think about it, I remember hearing him say he was going. I think his parents were

128

sending him as a birthday present or something. It isn't the kind of place that appeals to me, all that dry heat and boring blue sky, carrying water everywhere you go so you don't dehydrate. I'd rather have the changes of season here in New York."

"Wasn't there someone on that corridor from Arizona?"

"Steven Millman. Right. I don't remember which city—"

"Phoenix. That's where Heinz flew to."

"I assume you've spoken to him."

"Steven Millman practically doesn't exist, Mr. McHugh."

"Call me Marty, OK? In my business, the only people who call me *mister* work for people who work for me."

"I'm Chris, and no one works for me."

"Sounds like a good life. Why doesn't he exist?"

"I wish I knew. The last address on record is his parents' when he was at Rimson. He dropped out of the college the summer that Heinz died."

Marty McHugh looked at me as though I had said something intriguing. "Do tell. And no one answers his phone?"

"His mother, but she says she isn't sure if she can find him."

"Son of a bitch." He drank some more wine and looked out the window. We had a lovely day, a blue, almost cloudless sky, the sun hitting the Hudson River in a blinding splash of light. "I'll find him for you. I'll need a couple of days."

129

His statement stunned me. "How will you do that?"

He gave me a smile. "I have my ways. Ever hear of six degrees of separation? I have a Rolodex that connects me to the whole world. I'll get you Steve Millman."

"He may have changed his name," I said.

"Just adds to the fun."

"You seem to be an amazing man," I said.

"Seem to be? When I hand you Steve Millman on a silver platter, you'll know how amazing I am."

I laughed. I hadn't known what to expect from this man, but being entertained was not high on the list.

"So your theory is that Millman met Heinz in Arizona, they went hiking and Heinz fell, or—" He stopped. "Or what?"

"That's what I'd like to know. It may have been a simple accident, but whoever was with him—and I'm convinced someone was with him—didn't report the fall, stole some of his possessions, and sent one of the two suitcases back to the Gruners."

"I never liked Millman," Marty McHugh said.

"Why?"

"Snotty bastard. Know-it-all. You wouldn't have liked him, either." Marty pulled a leather agenda out of an inside jacket pocket and made a note with one of those big fat fancy black fountain pens.

"What did you think of Herb Fallon?" I asked. I wasn't looking for negative comments. I just wanted to know where his opinion fell regarding the person on the corridor with whom I'd had the most dealings.

"Nice guy. Honest. Good sense of humor." He grinned. "Like me."

"Thank you for the self-analysis." I was enjoying the conversation even more than the food.

We returned to the smaller room to select our hot dishes. From the repartee, it was clear that Martin McHugh was a regular here. The goodwill of the staff spilled over onto me, and I was coaxed into sampling far more than I had intended.

Back at our window table, I said, "I learned something yesterday that Heinz's mother found deeply upsetting." I went on to describe the cache of letters and quoted the lines about K.

"Interesting. And she wouldn't talk about it?"

"She practically threw me out of her room. She became frantic. Whoever this K person was, she refused to acknowledge knowing him, but it was perfectly clear that she did."

"K." He rested his chin on his hands, making grumbling sounds as he thought. "Winter, you said?"

"Winter."

"I knew a kid named Ken something."

"I don't think this was a kid. I don't think it was someone who was regularly on campus."

"Or he wouldn't have written home about it. You're right. Rimson was a small enough school that in a week, you ran into everyone you knew."

"Someone may have seen them together. They shook hands when they said good-bye."

"Not what undergrads did at Rimson. You shook

hands with a visitor, an older person, maybe with your father if you had that kind of relationship. K. You're not leaving all that food over?"

"It's a lot to eat, Marty."

"The chef'll be upset." He smiled. "They're saving berries and whipped cream for us."

"Oh my." I took another bite. It really was a shame to leave anything so good uneaten. "I don't suppose that Rolodex of yours has a card for Mr. K?"

"Not yet. But hey, we're just beginning."

We walked to Fifth Avenue together when the glorious meal had ended. There Marty turned north and I continued one long block to my garage. I drove home wondering whether his promises were bravado or if he really intended to make an effort to find Steve Millman. I didn't think there was any chance he could locate K. But if he was in touch with enough former classmates, Millman might surface.

I thought about the plagiarism charge he had endured. In my teaching during the years since I'd left St. Stephen's Convent, I'd encountered one serious case. It had happened in my poetry class, the class I taught before my current one. The style of writing had been so blatant, it had nearly slapped me in the face. The student was a girl who previously had barely been able to put together a complete sentence. Suddenly she was writing sentences that flowed with vocabulary I could not believe were part of her language: deft comparisons, clever figures of speech, even cleverer arguments to prove her point. No one else in the class had a paper in any way resembling hers, and when I had a private conversation with her, she broke down in tears.

I wondered what kind of impression Martin McHugh had made on the professor who charged him but not the real offender. Considering that he belonged to an expensive club and used its facilities regularly, I thought Rimson had lost a potentially generous donor.

There were no messages. I had been hoping that Mrs. Gruner would call to reopen our acquaintance. Who on earth could Mr. Kafka have been that she would react so stunningly? I changed from my black suit to my everyday casual clothes and went to pick Eddie up at his after-school activity. He was part of a group of children who were painting a backdrop for a forthcoming school play. From the look of his hands, I could see he had indulged freely in the paint.

"Are your hands dry?" I asked after we had kissed.

"I washed them with soap. The teacher made us. And I dried them, too." He climbed into his seat and got belted in.

"That's some project you're working on, Eddie."

"It's fun. Everybody has a color. Mine is dark blue."

His hands indicated more than one color. "Where did the red come from?"

"I helped Sandy. She couldn't reach high enough."

"That was very nice of you. But I think you'll have to wash again when we get home."

"OK," my son said breezily. It was all part of a day's work.

• • •

After the scrub-down, Eddie went to do his home-work and I went back to my list of Rimson students. Andrew Franklin, the Minneapolis lawyer, had suggested I call Arthur Howell, who had been Steven Millman's roommate. I thought that was a good place to continue my search. If anyone would know what a young man was doing on his vacation, it would be his roommate.

Arthur Howell answered his own phone, and I gave him a brief explanation of who I was. Then I said, "I wonder if you have a current address and phone number for your former roommate, Steven Millman."

There were several seconds of silence. Then, "Is this a joke?"

"Excuse me?" I looked at my list. "Is this Arthur Howell?"

"It is and you're the second person to call me with that question this afternoon."

So Martin McHugh had decided to call the obvious person. "I had lunch with Martin McHugh today," I explained. "He said he would try to find Steve Millman. I didn't know he had decided to call you. I'm sorry if I've bothered you."

"Just a surprise to hear that name twice in one afternoon. I didn't mean to upset you, Miss Bennett. I'll tell you what I told Marty. Steve and I were roommates, but we were never friends. I didn't really like the guy. It was because of the room lottery that we ended up together. I had a high number, he had a low one, and we

134

were talking one night the year before and decided to give rooming together a try. It was a mistake, but we survived it."

"Do you have a moment to talk about him?"

"Sure. What can I tell you?"

"Was he friendly with Heinz Gruner?"

"I'm not sure Millman was friends with anyone. He was an annoying creature, at least to me. He got on my nerves; probably got on lots of people's nerves."

"What did he major in?" I asked.

"History, I think."

"So did Heinz. So they probably knew each other from classes as well as from the dorm."

"A reasonable conclusion," Arthur Howell said. "It was a small school. We all knew each other."

"I understand he came from Phoenix."

"Right. He talked about it a lot. He loved it. He said it had the best weather in the world."

"You know that Heinz died in a hiking accident between Phoenix and Tucson."

"I heard later that summer. Can you tell me specifically what it is you're looking for?"

"I'm trying to find out who went hiking with Heinz Gruner."

"How do you know anyone did?"

I went through it again, the missing suitcases and backpack, the small backpack that disappeared and reappeared, the bits of evidence I had put together.

"Heinz was kind of a quiet guy," Arthur Howell said. "I remember hearing him talk about wanting to go to

135

Arizona in the spring, wanting to walk in the mountains. The feeling I got was that he went alone."

"Were you still in the dorm when he left?"

"I was the last man out of there. I had a lot of finals to take and one huge paper that I thought I'd never finish." He laughed. "They started to threaten me that they would lock up the dorm with me in it if I didn't clear out."

"I hope you did well," I said.

"I did, but it was a struggle. Probably the best paper I ever wrote."

"When did your roommate leave?"

"Let's see."

I knew it was a terrible question so many years later. I could not have answered it myself.

"He left before me, that's for sure. I'd say I was alone on that corridor for two days, worrying that they'd shut off the water and electricity." He laughed again. "I can't give you a date because I don't know what the dates of that last week were. It was May, that's all I know. I was sitting at my desk, trying to put together that paper, and Steve said he was leaving. I said good-bye hardly even looking up. It was such a relief to have that room to myself, even with all the trash he left."

"Do you have any recollection if he left around the same time as Heinz?"

"None. I'm sorry."

"When did you find out he wasn't returning to Rimson in the fall?"

136

"When I got to campus. We didn't keep in touch over the summer. I just realized one day I hadn't seen him and I asked someone, and was told he'd dropped out. Are you trying to tie that in with Heinz's accident?"

"I'm just trying to see if there's a connection."

"Well, I have to say I didn't like Millman, but I don't think he had anything to do with Heinz's death."

"Any idea how I can find him?"

"I gave Marty McHugh some phone numbers, but they may be dead ends. I haven't seen or heard from the guy since that morning at Rimson."

I asked him about K, and he came up blank. I wrote down the names he said he had given Marty McHugh. One of them was a girl whom Steve Millman had gone out with, a freshman that year. Arthur Howell had run into her at a convention he'd attended a couple of years back. She was married and working on Wall Street. I thought I might wait a few days to give Marty a head start. Now that I knew he was working on my behalf, I was sure I'd hear back from him.

"You ever room with anyone again?" I asked when our conversation was winding down.

"Not till I met my wife. She's a great roommate. I hope to keep her happy for the rest of our lives."

I smiled, wondering if he shared the compliment with his wife.

14

"So how was lunch?" my husband asked as he came inside the house. He has a knack of getting to what's important in life.

"It was much more than I expected, in every way. And my host, Martin McHugh, is a character. I have a feeling he may dig up the missing Mr. Millman."

"Well, I checked him out today," Jack said, giving his son a hug and then commenting on the fingers that still showed signs of blue and red paint despite the cleanup. "If he ever broke a law, law enforcement doesn't know about it. I couldn't even locate a driver's license for him."

"Then he's changed his identity."

"Looks like it. He could be dead, you know."

That gave me a chill. "I don't think so. Herb Fallon talked to his mother. She said she didn't know if she could locate him. She didn't say he'd died."

"I found some Millmans around the country," Jack said, pulling a sheet of paper out of his briefcase. "There's a Stephen with a P-H, but no one spelled like yours. He certainly doesn't drive a car in Arizona. Or own one."

I set the table as we were talking. I wasn't eating anything that night except a piece of melon. I felt as though I had just finished that huge lunch, even though it was hours before. I could still taste the fluffy texture of the whipped cream that came with the berries.

We talked about it again after Eddie had gone to bed. I looked at Jack's list of Millmans, not sure I wanted to call people around the country. His mother had to know where he was, and by this time she had probably talked to him and told him Herb Fallon was looking for him. Maybe I should have called, I thought. Herb came across as intimidating. Mrs. Millman might have decided not to pass along the message.

Two men on Dean Hershey's list had not yet been contacted. One lived in California and the other in Chicago, but I was too tired to make any more calls. It would have to wait till the next day.

Herb Fallon called in the morning, anxious to hear about my lunch with Marty McHugh. When I started describing the food, he interrupted. "Not the lunch, Chris. The *lunch*. What did Marty say?"

I switched to substance, embarrassed that I had thought he wanted to hear about the fare. I told him about my call to Arthur Howell, who had already heard from McHugh.

"So he's really on the ball," Herb said. "Sounds promising."

I told him that Jack hadn't found any trace of Millman.

"Maybe you should call the mother. You know, woman-to-woman. Maybe you can soften her up."

"I'll think about it. Right now I'd really like to see if I can patch things up with Mrs. Gruner."

"You may be able to make nice, but I bet she still

139

won't tell you anything about Kafka. It sounds as though that's a real stumbling block."

"It is. I wish I could think of a way to approach her."

"You'll work something out. Who's left on that corridor that we haven't talked to?"

I gave him the names.

"Jereth and Eric. Yeah. I think Eric went into linguistics, teaches at the University of Chicago. Jereth I'm not so sure."

"Well, I'll try to reach them today. And I'll think about how to approach Mrs. Gruner. I don't think anyone else can tell me about Mr. Kafka."

"He may not be relevant, you know. By the by, I did some digging yesterday. Looked up all the visiting speakers, musicians, dancers, you name it from that year. There are a few K's in there, a guitarist named Tom Klapp, a speaker named Keith Gordon. He had a book out on Japan as a leader of industry at the time he spoke. I'm pretty sure I went to his lecture. It put me to sleep. I looked over the speakers carefully. Considering who the Gruners were, they were more likely to pal around with intellectuals than guitarists."

"Anything interesting about this Keith Gordon?"

"It didn't seem so to me. And there were no speakers with a last name beginning with K."

"Well, you tried," I said.

We talked for a few more minutes, then hung up. I now had two more sources to contact and then I would hit a wall, unless these men could tell me something new. The information I needed was Steve Millman's address or the name of the person who'd hiked with Heinz Gruner.

What troubled me the most was the sense that one of the very nice men who had lived on Heinz's corridor that year had lied to me. They were all so kind and helpful on the telephone and in person, as in the case of Martin McHugh. Had an expensive lunch covered up the fact that he had killed Heinz Gruner, either accidentally or purposefully? Was it possible that Herb Fallon, who had helped me the most, had been the other man on the mountain? Or any of the other people who had denied going to Arizona?

Andrew Franklin from Minneapolis claimed he had helped Heinz down the stairs with his suitcases to a taxi, then gone back up again. What if Franklin had hopped into the same taxi and taken off for Phoenix?

I had listened to each man's story and believed it. But the truth was, any one of them could be a viable suspect.

I looked at the last two names on my list and decided to call Eric Goode, the man in Chicago, which was one hour earlier than the East Coast.

He answered his phone on the first ring. I gave him my standard introduction.

"You're talking about something that happened almost twenty years ago."

"That's right."

"You really expect me to remember what day or date I left Rimson that spring?"

"Anything that you remember will be helpful. Can

you tell me where you went when you left the college?"

"Home. Where else?"

"I thought you might have joined Heinz Gruner in Arizona."

"We weren't what you'd call friends. We lived on the same corridor, but that was it."

"Do you remember anyone going to Arizona with him?"

"Honestly? I don't even remember Gruner going. The first I knew he'd gone was when I heard he'd died down there."

"When did you hear?"

"I don't know. Maybe someone called me during the summer. I really don't remember."

This was going nowhere, and he sounded put upon. "Do you know if Heinz had a friend or acquaintance who visited him during the winter of that year? A man older than a student?"

Eric Goode chuckled. "I told you already. I didn't really know the guy. I don't know who he was friends with."

"Did you know Steve Millman?"

"Steve? Yes. He was next door to me that year. Had a roommate, Artie Howell, I think."

"Do you recall when Steve left for home?"

"No."

"How about his roommate?"

"No idea."

I wrapped it up, giving him my usual information in case he remembered anything, which I knew he

142

wouldn't. This had been my least successful conversation thus far. He didn't know, he didn't remember, he didn't especially care.

I tried to decide whether to call Mrs. Gruner, to drive over and knock on her door, or to wait to hear from her. I didn't want to arrive at her door only to be told to leave. That would signal the end of our relationship, if it hadn't already ended with our last meeting.

Looking around for a diversion, I spied the three names Arthur Howell had given me, people who might know where to find Steve Millman. One of them was Liz Clark, née Baldwin. I dialed her number in New York. I wanted to hear a woman's voice and a woman's point of view after all the men I had spoken to.

"This is Liz," a clear voice said.

"Mrs. Clark, my name is Chris Bennett," and I went on with my canned intro. "The person I'm trying to locate is Steve Millman. I believe you used to know him."

"Marty McHugh called and asked the same question yesterday. I take it you're the person he was referring to."

"Probably. What can you tell me?"

"Well, I actually heard from Steve after he left Rimson."

"You did? When was that?"

"Several times, actually. He had a thing for me and whenever he felt particularly happy or depressed, he'd reach for the phone and give me a call. That went on for several years."

She had ignited my waning enthusiasm. "Tell me about the calls. Where did they come from? What was he doing? Did you ever get together with him?"

Liz Clark laughed. "Marty McHugh got pretty excited, too, when I told him. Steve didn't always tell me where he was and I never tried to call him back, but I don't think he was in Phoenix. No, I *know* he wasn't in Phoenix. He took a year off after he dropped out of Rimson."

"Do you know why he dropped out?"

"Something happened. He never said what, but I assumed it was a family thing. His father's business may have suffered some problems. The money may have dried up. I'm just speculating."

"Go on. What did he do after that year?"

"He got his degree somewhere else, maybe the University of Arizona, I'm not sure. He was never very clear about what he was doing."

"I assume he went to work somewhere?" I asked.

"Yes, but he was vague about that, too. And I have to tell you something. I think he changed his name."

Not exactly a surprise. "To what?"

"I have no idea. It was something he said, that I wouldn't be able to find him if I tried to call. Not that I ever called him. He initiated all the calls. I just talked. I think he wanted to lose himself."

"Do you know why?"

"Not a clue."

"Do you know that a student on his corridor that last year died in a mountain climb that summer?" I asked.

144

"I heard about it when I got back to Rimson in the fall. They had a memorial service. I've forgotten the name but I know it was someone Steve knew. Do you think there's some connection between Steve leaving Rimson and that fellow getting killed?"

"I don't know, but I'm trying to find out."

"Marty McHugh didn't say anything about that."

That meant he was a careful interrogator. "Did Steve have a lot of friends at Rimson?"

She didn't answer for a moment. "That's a tough one. I'm not sure I can answer it. Steve was a guy who complained about people. Not about me; he really liked me. But he had gripes about lots of guys he knew. His roommate annoyed him. That's not unusual. This guy said something nasty, that guy didn't pay back the ten dollars Steve lent him. I never heard him say nice things about people. Maybe that's why I was hesitant to keep the relationship going."

"I don't suppose you remember the names of the people he complained about," I said hopefully.

"It's so long ago. These were tales about people I didn't know. I wish I could help you."

"Did he ever say anything about hiking in Arizona at the end of the semester, maybe with a friend?"

"He could have," Liz Clark said. "I remember we were out, maybe just having a coffee or a beer, and we got to talking about hitchhiking in Europe and mountain climbing in India, and he said something about not having to go far from home when you lived in Arizona. There were lots of places to hike and climb. I don't remember clearly where the conversation went from there, but he could have mentioned that he was going to do that."

Could have mentioned. "Did you tell Marty McHugh that?"

"He didn't ask. He just wanted to find out where Steve was living or working."

"Mrs. Clark, if you recall any conversation about Steve hiking in Arizona at the end of that year, would you call me?"

"Sure thing."

I gave her my info, thanked her for being helpful, and finished our conversation. I was on my way upstairs when I heard the phone ring. I dashed back and picked it up.

"Mrs. Brooks?" It was a man.

"Yes."

"This is Dr. Farley. I'm on staff at Hillside Village."

"Oh."

"I was talking to Mrs. Gruner a little while ago. She seemed quite distressed, and we had a talk. Apparently you and she had become friendly recently. Is that true?"

"Yes, it is."

"And something happened the last time you visited."

I admitted that this was so but said nothing more about it.

"Whatever happened, Mrs. Gruner has been adversely affected by it. Are you aware of this?"

"I am, and I'm very sorry. She told me to leave and it seemed quite final. I had hoped she might change her mind."

"She has, but she doesn't know how to tell you. Are you free this morning?"

"Yes, I am."

"If you'd like to run over to Hillside Village in the next hour, perhaps I can mediate an end to your dispute."

"I'll be very glad to come, Dr. Farley. This was not a dispute and I have no ill feelings for Mrs. Gruner. Quite the opposite."

"Come on over. The desk will call me when you arrive."

I straightened up the house and drove over to Hillside Village.

15

The woman at the desk was expecting me. She made a quick phone call and told me to walk down the hall to room 107. The door was ajar, and I went in. It was a small room with comfortable furniture where a family could sit and talk without being overheard or interrupted. No one was there. Just as I sat in a chair, the door was pushed open and a man in a white medical coat walked in.

"Mrs. Brooks?"

I stood. "Yes."

"I'm Dr. Farley. We have a few minutes before Mrs.

Gruner arrives. Would you like to tell me what happened last week?"

I did it as briefly as I could, explaining that I was researching Mrs. Gruner's son's death almost twenty years before, that she had given me the letters, and that I had asked her about K.

"She became very upset," I said. "She said she wouldn't talk about it and asked me to leave. I did. She was quite angry."

As I finished speaking, the door was pushed all the way open and Mrs. Gruner, in a wheelchair, was propelled into the room. The aide left, closing the door. I went to the wheelchair, offering Mrs. Gruner my hand and wishing her a good morning.

She hesitated, but took my hand and nodded, her eyes averted. I returned to my chair. Dr. Farley sat on the sofa so that he faced both of us. He smiled warmly at Mrs. Gruner, and his "mediation" began. He encouraged me to say I was sorry I had upset her and she acknowledged that she had acted intemperately but had no desire to break off our friendship. Still, it was very important that I not bring up that painful topic again.

I assured her I would not.

There wasn't much more left to discuss. When Dr. Farley was satisfied that he had successfully mended our relationship, he assured us we could remain in the room as long as we wanted. Then he was on his way.

When the door closed, I said. "It's very nice out, Mrs. Gruner. We could take a ride. Maybe you'd like to have lunch out."

"Not today," she said. "I'm very tired. I didn't sleep well last night. Maybe another day. I think after my lunch, I will try to sleep this afternoon."

I could see the hollows under her eyes. Whether our unfortunate spat—or something worse—had been the cause of her sleeplessness, I could not determine. What I realized was that I could no longer talk to her about Heinz because it would remind her of K and her anger. I would have to keep our relationship on a more superficial and much less interesting level.

"I hope that will help," I said.

"Everything makes me tired now. I remember when I was an energetic woman, when I worked and had interesting thoughts. Now . . ." Her voice faded.

"You're just tired," I assured her. I looked at my watch. It was nearly lunch hour. "Let me take you to the dining room."

"Thank you."

I pushed the chair into the hall and down to the dining room. People were already moving toward it. As we reached the door, Mrs. Gruner raised herself and stood, holding her cane.

"I like to walk when I can. Just leave the chair. Someone will come for it."

"I'll see you next week, Mrs. Gruner."

"Yes. I will rest over the weekend."

I was not heartened by our meeting. If the mention of K a couple of days before had done all this to her—kept her from sleeping, made her listless—he had to be very important in the life of her family. And it seemed that our former relationship had ended. We could no longer talk about the subject that had brought us together. We would have to limit our subject matter to the weather and perhaps gossip.

Saddened, I drove home. It was noon and I wanted to call Jereth Phillips in California.

Except for him and Steve Millman, I had now spoken to every man on Heinz's corridor. Everyone had denied having gone to Arizona that year. I pulled out a piece of paper and grabbed a pencil. Liz Clark had said that Steve "could have mentioned" that he was going to hike in Arizona.

Prof. Herb Fallon had gone home when his exams were over. He had heard about Heinz's death later in the summer.

Marty McHugh had gone home. He was working to find Steve Millman by calling people who might know where he was. Was it possible that he already knew where Steve was and would come back to me with an address and phone number that he presumably elicited from someone on my list, but which he'd had all along?

Barry Woodson, the lawyer, knew nothing of Heinz's trip to Arizona.

Andrew Franklin from Minnesota also knew nothing.

Arthur Howell, Steve's roommate, claimed to have been the last man out of the dorm, thus alibiing himself, although there were no witnesses to back him up.

I picked up the phone and dialed the number Dean Hershey had given me for Jereth Phillips.

"Phillips," a voice said on the first ring.

150

"Mr. Phillips, my name is Christine Bennett." I went on with my practiced intro. "Do you recall the students on your corridor that year?" I ended.

"Most of them, yeah. I certainly remember Heinz Gruner and Herb Fallon. Heinz is the one who died."

"Yes, just after the spring semester. He flew to Arizona to do some hiking. Do you recall that?"

"I think I heard them talking about that."

"Who else talked about it?"

"What's his name, Millman, the guy from Phoenix. They were going down together."

"They were? I didn't know anyone went with Heinz."

"Millman went. He lived down there. He said he could show Heinz some good places to hike."

"Did you get the feeling then that they were going to hike together?"

"That's what it sounded like. I wasn't part of the trip so I just heard bits and pieces. But I think they left together."

"So you were still in the dorm when they took off?"

"I probably had another exam or two. It's a long time ago. I can't be sure."

"Did anyone else go with them?"

"I couldn't tell you."

"When did you hear about Heinz's accident?"

"Hmm." He hummed something tuneless. "Couldn't tell you. I'm pretty sure I knew before I got back to Rimson in the fall. Maybe Herb called. Yeah, I think he did."

"Herb Fallon?"

"That's the one. He's on the faculty at Rimson now. You could give him a call there."

We finished our conversation soon after. I had the feeling that this man was telling me the whole truth. Maybe it was because he had implicated Steve Millman, which no one else had done. But if Heinz and Millman had gone to the airport together, then Andrew Franklin's story of helping Heinz downstairs with his luggage and depositing him in an empty taxi was beginning to fray. Something wasn't right. If Millman and his luggage were already in the taxi, Franklin would have seen either the person or his luggage, or both.

I set aside the papers, made some lunch, and ate it with the *Times* at my elbow. I had completed the first round of phone calls and had no idea whether there would be another round. Asking these men similar questions would surely elicit similar answers. But I had new information, tentative information from Liz Clark and certain information from Jereth Phillips that Steve Millman had gone to Arizona with Heinz—which might put Millman on Picacho Peak with Heinz a day later.

I put a red asterisk next to Jereth Phillips's name. I was sure he was telling me the truth.

I was about to call Herb Fallon with my new piece of information when the phone rang. It was the mother of Terry, one of Eddie's friends. She could not pick him up today. Could I bring him to my home, and she would drop by between four and five? She'd let the school know.

I was rather pleased at the opportunity to repay what I considered a motherly debt. Eddie visited his friends after school more than they visited him at our house. One of them had a pool, which made his house much more inviting. I gathered the papers from the Heinz Gruner case, put them on the dining room table, and reverted to my other persona.

Saturday is father-and-son day. I generally sleep a little later than usual and come downstairs to muffins, occasionally freshly baked, and whatever else Jack wants to scrape up for breakfast. When we finished eating, Jack and Eddie took off for the hardware store. I think Eddie will grow up believing that there is no life on Saturday without a visit to some kind of hardware store. Today they intended to drop by a garden supply store as well. Our lawn needed some greening up and our hose needed a new washer. They would take care of everything.

I was cleaning up the kitchen when the phone rang.

"Mrs. Brooks?"

"Yes."

"This is Dr. Farley at Hillside Village."

"Yes, good morning."

"I'm afraid I have bad news for you."

I felt my heart tighten. "What happened?"

"Mrs. Gruner died in her sleep."

"Oh no." I sat down, feeling panicky. "How?"

"It looks as though she may have had another stroke. I don't think she was in pain. Yours is the only name I have as a friend. Her family is gone, as you know, and whatever friends she had outside Hillside Village, she never put them on the list of people to be informed."

"I'm so sorry to hear it. Is there anything I can do? What will happen to her?"

"She left instructions. She'll be buried next to her husband and son."

I felt tearful. I held the phone away and tried to overcome the tightening of my throat.

"Mrs. Brooks?"

"Yes. I'm sorry. It's just such a shock. She seemed to be doing so well."

"She appreciated your visits, you know. Whatever that little problem was a few days ago, I think you worked it out successfully. This was something we always knew might happen."

"What will you do with her things?"

"There isn't much, and there are no heirs. Her clothes will be given away. I think she had a watch and a few pieces of jewelry. If there's something you'd like to have—"

"There's nothing, thank you. I just—" My mind had begun functioning again. "I'd like to see her collection of papers before you throw them out."

"That won't be a problem. Why don't you drop over at your convenience? The room is empty and you can go through them alone."

I told him I would do that. I hung up and remained sitting on my chair, thinking of the poor woman whose life had ended as quietly as she had lived it. The tragedy was that she had lost her family and renounced her friends. I hoped I had convinced her that her son had not committed suicide. That was the information she had been living for.

I left a note for Jack on the kitchen counter. My appetite had deserted me, and the thought of lunch held no appeal.

Dr. Farley was still at Hillside Village when I got there. He had doffed the white coat and was preparing to leave. I assumed he had been called when Mrs. Gruner's body had been discovered. We shook hands and he said a few nice words, then sent me up to Mrs. Gruner's room with an aide who unlocked the door and left.

The bed had been stripped. Clothes hung in the closet, shoes lay on the floor, and her worn black leather handbag rested on top of the dresser. I closed the door and sat down on the guest chair with the pocketbook. Inside was a wallet with some cash in it, a single credit card, insurance cards including Medicare, and several old photos that I took to be of her, her husband, and her young son. Even as a child, Heinz's face was recognizable. She had been a plain woman, but her hair had been dark and combed attractively, her dress fit her well, and her smile lit up her face.

Tissues, keys, cough drops, and a small address book took up most of the rest of the space. I pulled out the address book and flipped to K. There were listings for Alfred Koch, Maria Kramer, and Paul Kristen. All had addresses and phone numbers. The address for Maria Kramer was in Germany. I put the book in my bag and went to the closet where I remembered the carton of letters was.

Moving the carton to the bed, I saw that the letters were divided and rubber-banded. The pack that I had looked at earlier in the week contained letters from Heinz to his parents. Another group was letters from his parents to him. Obviously, he had been as sentimental as his mother, saving his parents' missives. Mrs. Gruner must have found them among his things after he died and put them with the others. A quick look told me they were dated his last week at college.

Next, I went through the dresser drawers. All I found were underclothes, sweaters, and stockings. But having learned from my expert husband, I emptied one of the two top drawers, pulled it all the way out, and inverted it on top of the bed. Nothing. I replaced it, refilled it, and did the same to the drawer beside it. Taped to the bottom was a small envelope.

I pulled it off the wood and opened it. Inside was a key that looked like the key to our box in our local bank. Sure enough, a small piece of paper named the bank and the box number.

I was in a quandary. This did not belong to me. I could imagine why Mrs. Gruner had taped it to the bottom of the drawer, probably one of the only two drawers she was strong enough to pull out and invert by herself. Worrying that someone might rummage through her dresser when she was out of the room, she

156

kept it hidden. How she expected anyone to find it was a mystery to me.

It occurred to me then that once a year the bank would send a bill for the box, and perhaps someone at Hillside Village would go hunting for the key. I put the key in my purse, intending to call Dr. Farley or someone else in the building to let them know of the key's existence.

Then I returned to the carton. I wanted to go through every envelope, and that would take me a longer time than I had to spend in the room. I called down to the front desk and asked if I could take the carton home with me. I would be glad to bring it back if anyone wanted it.

The woman who answered said she would call me back at Mrs. Gruner's number. While I waited, I looked more carefully through the closet but found nothing of interest. I even put my hand into the pockets of dresses and coats but came out with nothing more than what I might find in my own: tissues, notes to remember to buy something, gloves, a few coins.

The woman downstairs called back and said I could have the carton. She would send a wheelchair up to the room; I could use that to get the carton downstairs. If I was ready to leave, she would have someone lock the door behind me. I said I was ready and gathered everything I was taking into the carton. When the volunteer came with the wheelchair, I piled it on and walked to the elevator.

157

16

What I had was the consolidated memory of a family of three. That so many years, so many thoughts, so many events could be crowded into a single carton astonished and saddened me. Jack helped me carry the carton into the house and stashed it in our dining room. When I was able, meaning when I was alone, I would scan the letters, both to and from Heinz, and see if I could find a reference to K. And I would try to call the two men in the address book whose names began with that letter.

It wasn't until Sunday afternoon, when Jack took Eddie and my cousin Gene out for a drive, that I was able to attack the contents of the carton. I remembered approximately where the letter referring to K had been located and I found it. Apparently Mrs. Gruner had not removed or destroyed it. I reread it, learning nothing new.

I then read deeper into the past, skimming the letters for another reference to the man, but finding none. The time of these letters was already the year before Heinz died, so there would be nothing referring to his last hike.

Finally, I took the package of letters that had been written to Heinz. His parents were not his only correspondents. I found a letter from a high school teacher whose name I recognized, apparently responding to some questions Heinz had asked him. It didn't seem relevant to my pursuit. A letter from Herb Fallon during the summer between their freshman and sophomore years described a boring but well-paying job. A postcard from Mike Borden, a name that did not ring a bell, had been sent from France. The picture was of the quay at Marseilles, a line of restaurants advertising seafood. "Get yourself over here" was the gist of the message.

I went further back in time. The letters from his parents were not easy to read. They were written in a distinct European handwriting that required deciphering, and in the end nothing of importance to me was in them.

And then a typewritten letter leaped out at me. The return address carried the name A. Koch, one of the names listed in Mrs. Gruner's address book. It was dated the spring of Heinz's freshman year.

I hope you're working as hard and successfully as I know you can. Your first-semester grades were good and I expect your second-semester grades will be even better. You are certainly shining in history and I think your plan of majoring in that area is wise. Your parents tell me that you are enjoying your experience at Rimson, as you should. It's as fine a college as you will find anywhere and the faculty rivals even the best universities in the country. The smaller student body is, in my opinion, more conducive to study than the institutions with populations the size of cities.

Feel free to call or write at any time. Keep up the good work.

It was signed with a scribble that I interpreted as Alfred Koch. The inside address was the west side of Manhattan, giving no affiliation. It was almost certainly a residence. I resisted the urge to call him—the phone number was in the address book—as Jack and company might return at any moment. But I was convinced that this was the elusive K whom Heinz had mentioned. From the content of the letter, I had to assume he was somehow involved in Heinz's education, or at least in his choice of Rimson over other schools. This puzzled me. It was my observation that Heinz could have had his pick of schools. The tone of the letter indicated he might have wanted Harvard or Yale but that Mr. Koch had dissuaded him. Having happily attended a small institution myself, I could second that opinion.

The door opened and feet and voices poured into the house. I went to greet my family and offer them some ice cream. K would have to wait another day.

Monday morning, after the men had left, I made the phone call. A woman answered and asked me to wait. After a silence, a voice said, "This is Alfred Koch."

"Yes, good morning," I said. "My name is Christine Bennett and I am a friend of Mrs. Hilda Gruner."

"Hilda, yes. Has something happened?"

"I'm sorry to tell you she died of a stroke over the weekend."

He expressed his surprise and sympathy. He had spoken to her several months before and had heard nothing more.

"Mr. Koch, I was a classmate of Heinz Gruner in high school. I've been looking into the circumstances of his death almost twenty years ago."

"It was very tragic, Miss Bennett. He was young and had a promising life ahead of him. He died of an apparent fall in the Southwest. His parents' lives were shattered. His father died a year or so later. Hilda had a stroke. I'm sure you know the story."

"I do, and I've been learning that not all of the story is factual."

"I don't know what you mean by that."

"He was hiking with someone, perhaps a friend from Rimson College, a person who never reported the accident."

"How do you know this?"

"I've been speaking to the people who found his body and to the students who lived on his corridor at Rimson that year."

"What is your interest in this, Miss Bennett?"

"Just a search for the truth. At first, I hoped to establish that Heinz had not committed suicide. Then—"

"It was clearly an accident," Koch interrupted. "What would make you think it was otherwise?" He sounded like a lawyer cross-examining a reluctant witness.

"Several things," I retorted. "But I called you to ask you what your relationship was with Heinz."

161

That stopped him for a few seconds. "Why do you want to know that?"

"Because he mentioned you in a letter to his parents, and one of his friends saw you with him on campus."

"My relationship with Heinz Gruner had nothing to do with his death. It had to do with his life."

Very cute, I thought. "Still, it's a dangling fact. Since all the participants are now dead, I would hope you could tell me and let me be the judge of its relevance."

Another silence. "I have no obligation to you, Miss Bennett."

"That's true. But I have an obligation to learn the full story of the end of Heinz Gruner's life. I hope you'll help me do that."

"I have to think about it."

"If you'd like the phone number of the residence where Mrs. Gruner lived and died, I can give it to you."

"I have it, thank you. Give me yours, if I decide to get back to you."

I dictated the number. He took it and ended the conversation.

I was annoyed. He was right that he had no obligation to tell me anything, but I felt he could have been more forthcoming. I went upstairs to the computer and searched for his name. I had not done this before, but Jack had listed the websites that would be helpful. I found Alfred Koch on the first try. He was a professor of European history at Columbia University, which was a brisk walk or a short bus or subway ride north of where he lived. He was apparently an immigrant from

162

Germany, but at an early age. His English had no hint of an accent. I assumed that his ties to the Gruners might go back to their native country.

According to the listing, he was a full professor, had received numerous awards, and was the author of several scholarly books. I looked carefully through his biography and found that he had taught at Rimson College about thirty years before. So that was a connection. I wrote down his Columbia office address and phone number. I did not intend to wait until he decided to call me back. I wanted to know what his relationship with Heinz was, although I was beginning to have some ideas.

A few minutes later I received a call from Hillside Village. Mrs. Gruner's funeral had been arranged to take place at the village on Tuesday morning at ten so that all the residents who wished to could attend. There would also be transportation to the cemetery. I thought about calling Alfred Koch back to tell him, but decided he knew how to dial as well as I.

Instead, I called Dean Hershey at Rimson and asked for the phone number of the student who had sent Heinz the postcard from Marseilles. He put me on hold and came back with it. Michael Borden lived in Boston.

"He's a hospital administrator," Hershey said. "An MD. Where'd you come up with his name?"

I told him and let him know that Mrs. Gruner had died, concluding the call. I was pleased to have this new contact. A friend who had not been part of the dorm corridor might know whom Heinz had traveled to Arizona with and might give me a name.

I then called Dr. Farley and told him of my discovery of the key taped to the dresser drawer.

"Thank you very much, Mrs. Brooks. I'm the executor of Mrs. Gruner's will and I might have gone nuts looking for that key. I do have a copy of her will. Have you heard about the funeral?"

"I have and I'll be there. I can bring the key with me."

"Fine. And then perhaps you'll accompany me to the bank to open the box. I'd like to have a witness with me."

I assured him that I would be happy to do that, and we left the time open.

The phone rang while I was making a shopping list.

"Chris, this is Marty McHugh."

"Hello. This is a surprise."

"Why? I thought you wanted me to locate Steve Millman."

"Yes, but—well, what have you got?"

"I found him."

"You did?"

"Took a little doing, some phone calls, some prodding, but I've got your man."

I grabbed a fresh piece of paper and poised the pencil I'd been using to make my shopping list. "Go."

"Well, I can't give you his number. I spoke to him yesterday and he won't allow it. What we can do is the following: I'll phone him and then conference you in. You'll have to ask all your questions with me on the line."

"That's acceptable. When would you like to do it?"

He read off some time periods that Steve would be available, the earliest of which was that afternoon, which made me think that Millman was out west. That would be the start of his lunch hour.

"Three is fine for me," I said before he could go on. "Is that OK for you?"

"Fine. I'll call him, then call you. It may be a few minutes past the hour."

"I'll be here. Thank you, Marty. I really appreciate this."

"Happy to deliver."

What I was left wondering after I hung up was whether McHugh had had the number all along and had made the calls to Arthur Howell and Liz Clark—and possibly others—as show in case I checked up on him. But it didn't matter. I was going to talk to Steve Millman.

It was just short of noon when my shopping was completed, and I thought that would be a good time to call the man who had written the postcard from Marseilles two decades before.

"Borden," he answered on the first ring.

"Dr. Borden, my name is Christine Bennett. I was a classmate of Heinz Gruner in high school."

"Heinz! I haven't heard that name in years. Poor guy died hiking in the mountains before we graduated."

"I know. And I know you were his friend because he saved a postcard you sent him from Marseilles."

"That was a hell of a long time ago. What can I do for you?"

I went through it briefly. "Did you know his plans for flying to Arizona that year?" I finished.

"Oh yeah. We were good friends. We were going to room together that year but it didn't work out. I was upstairs from him. We talked about going to Arizona together but something came up. I think my cousin was getting married and the whole family was going. So I couldn't go with him."

"Who did go?"

"Oh, some guy in our class from Arizona. What was his name? Steve something. I think Heinz was going to stay with Steve's family the first night and they were driving to someplace where you could hike in the mountains and it wasn't too difficult. At least, that's what I heard."

"Dr. Borden, were you friends with any of the people on Heinz's corridor that year?"

"I knew a lot of them, but I wasn't friends with them."

"Do you know if anyone else on that corridor went to Arizona with Heinz and Steve?"

"No idea. I think Heinz wanted to go by himself, to tell you the truth, and Steve kind of wormed his way into his plans. I don't even know if they both went on the hike. But I'm pretty sure Heinz was staying the first night with the—what's their name? Millman. He was staying with the Millmans."

"Do you know that Steve never went back to Rimson after that year?"

"I heard. I figured he was really shook up by what happened."

"Were you ever in touch with Steve Millman after that?" I asked.

"Nah. We weren't friends."

"When did you hear about Heinz's accident?"

"You know, I called him during the summer. I wanted to know how the hiking went, and I'm not much of a letter writer. That card from France was about my limit. His father answered and told me what happened. I remember that he cried on the phone. I was shaking when I got off. I couldn't believe it."

"What did he tell you?"

"Just that there had been an accident, that Heinz was hiking on some mountain between Phoenix and Tucson, and he fell off the trail and down the side of the mountain and died."

"Did he say anything about who was with him?"

"Nothing, and I didn't ask. What was I—nineteen years old? I'm talking to my friend's father and he's crying over the phone and I can't even comprehend what he's telling me. I didn't want to keep that conversation going."

"Dr. Borden, you've been very helpful. Thank you." I gave him my name again and my phone number.

When I finished my lunch, I called Jack and told him what I'd learned.

"You're actually talking to him this afternoon?"

"Three o'clock. What would you ask him?"

"All the questions he won't answer. Was he there, was

167

he with Heinz when the accident happened, how did it happen, why did Millman walk off with the back-pack—you know the drill."

"I'll give it a try. Maybe after all this time, he's ready to come clean."

"Not if he was involved in the death. Even if they don't try him, he'll need a lawyer and it'll cost him, not just money but time. But who knows? You've cracked some tough ones before."

I smiled. "OK. Just wanted to keep you posted."

17

I felt excited at the prospect of the upcoming phone call. Jack was surely right that Millman would answer none of the important questions. He'd had twenty years to think about how to evade the truth and a few hours already that day to rehearse. I knew things he couldn't possibly know—in particular, that the young couple who'd spotted the body and the backpack had not seen the backpack on the way up. If Steve had been with Heinz, it was logical that he was the person who took it away and replaced it after sanitizing its contents. He also had to be the person who'd sent one suitcase to the Gruners.

I made a list of questions to ask him, putting the important ones up front. He might decide at any moment that he had heard enough and disconnect. Then he was lost to me forever. While I was writing the questions, the phone rang. It was Liz Clark,

Steve's wannabe girlfriend.

"You asked me to call you if I remembered anything about Steve and that hike in Arizona."

"Yes. What do you remember?"

"I'm sure he told me he was going. It wasn't just a maybe. He asked me to come to Phoenix and meet his parents and then we could go hiking. That really scared me."

"What scared you," I asked, "meeting his parents or hiking with him?"

She laughed. "Both, if you want the truth. But mostly meeting his parents. He was obviously more serious about me than I was about him. I told him I couldn't go."

"So what makes you think he was going to hike with a college friend?"

"After I said I couldn't make it, he groused around for a while. Then he said he'd be going anyway with some guy in the dorm. I don't think he mentioned a name."

I thanked her for taking the trouble to call. When I got off the phone, it was nearly three. I scribbled a few more questions that I knew I would never get to ask, and waited tensely for the phone to ring. Three o'clock came and went. I looked nervously at my watch. Nothing happened. Then the front door opened—I had left it open for Eddie—and the phone rang at the same moment.

"Come on in, honey," I called, then, into the phone, "Hello?"

There was a moment of pandemonium. I shushed Eddie, took out the milk, and responded to Marty McHugh's greeting. I put my finger to my lips to show Eddie he had to be quiet.

"Yes, I'm here, Marty. Sorry. My son just came home from school."

"You want me to call back?"

"No. I'm ready."

"OK. Go ahead. I have Steve on the line."

"Mr. Millman," I said, sliding into my chair and taking the waiting pencil. "My name is Christine Bennett Brooks and I am calling to talk to you about Heinz Gruner's death."

"I wasn't there," a second man's voice said. "I can't tell you anything about it."

"I've been told by several people who graduated from Rimson that you planned to join Heinz in Arizona for a hike."

"That's true," Steve Millman said. "I did plan it, but I backed out at the last minute."

"What happened?"

"My father arranged a job interview for me in Phoenix for the day we wanted to go down to Picacho Peak, and I couldn't break the appointment."

"What did Heinz do?" I asked.

"He went hiking without me."

"How did he get to Picacho Peak?"

"My mother said he rented a car."

"Do you remember what car rental company he used?"

170

There was a silent second. "Car rental company? Twenty years ago? I wasn't even in the house when he made the call."

"What happened to his suitcase?"

"What suitcase?"

"The one he took with him from Rimson."

"No idea. He must have taken it in the car. It wasn't in our house."

"So he packed up his belongings, rented a car, and drove away?"

"That's what happened. I think my mother made him a sandwich. She was that kind of mother."

"When did you find out about Heinz's death?"

"I don't remember. I think there was a piece in the paper about a body being found on Picacho Peak."

"Did you tell anyone?"

"Like who?"

I cringed slightly at his grammar. "Like the people you were friendly with at Rimson."

"It was a busy summer, Mrs. Brooks. I got that job and I worked my tail off."

"Mr. Millman, we've found new information on the circumstances of Heinz's death. He was definitely hiking with someone."

"So he met a guy in the parking lot. I don't know anything about it."

He was starting to annoy me. "And no one called your home about the rental car?"

"Not that I remember. Maybe the cops took care of it."

"They didn't. As far as they know, there wasn't any rental car."

"Look, you're trying to make me responsible for things I know nothing about. My information is that he rented a car. That's all I can tell you. And he took his luggage with him. He didn't leave anything at our house."

"Why did you drop out of Rimson?" I asked.

"For a lot of reasons. One, my job became permanent. Another is that I found out about Heinz and I felt pretty awful."

"Did anyone call to tell you?"

"Not that I remember. It's possible."

"Did you fly down to Phoenix with Heinz?"

"Uh, yeah, I think so."

"When you left the dorm, did you both ride to the airport in the same taxi?"

"Yes, we did. Dragged our suitcases down the stairs and got in a taxi."

"Was anyone else in that taxi?" I asked.

"There wasn't room. We had a lot of luggage between us. He took everything he had to Arizona. He was going home from there. There wasn't room for another suitcase in that cab. We were really loaded down."

I wasn't happy. He had ready answers and none of them matched what I already knew, or had been told. "When you heard that Heinz had died, did you call his parents to give them your condolences?"

Now the silence was longer. "I don't think so. Where is this going?"

"I'm trying to find out how and why he died," I said. "I knew him in high school. He was a nice person. He didn't deserve to die an early death. His death destroyed his parents. That's where this is going."

"Well, I wish you luck. If you find out what happened, let Marty know. He may be able to find me again. You have any other questions? I'm kind of busy."

"I have no more questions, Mr. Millman, but I'd like to tell you that I don't believe what you've told me. I think you were there on the mountain with Heinz. I don't think there was a rental car. I think he was driven to Picacho Peak by a friend and he left his suitcases in the friend's car. His death was a tragedy, but I'm not convinced it was accidental."

"What are you saying?"

"Someone was with him and witnessed the fall. That person removed the small backpack Heinz was carrying."

"How do you know this?"

"Because the backpack wasn't there when my witnesses went up the trail a day or so after his death, but it *was* there when they came down."

"Well, it sounds like you've found people who know a lot more about this than I do. I wish you luck. Marty, I'm hanging up. Thanks for arranging this." And he clicked off.

"You there, Chris?"

"Yes, I'm here."

"You get anything out of it?"

"Almost nothing that Steve told me matches what

I've been told by other people."

"So someone is lying."

"It would seem that way."

"And you think it's Steve."

"I do," I said. "If it isn't Steve, it has to be several other people."

"Which ones?"

I was about to name names and then I stopped. I had reached a point in this case where I didn't know whom to trust, and that included Marty McHugh, even though he had located Steve Millman for me and arranged this conversation. "I don't know, Marty," I said wearily. Eddie was tugging at my sleeve, trying to show me something. "How did you find him, by the way?"

"Just kept at it. I have a network of friends and associates that rivals the FBI."

I wasn't sure whether to believe that, either. "Well, I appreciate your help."

"Keep me on your radar, OK? If you find out anything, give me a call. I'd like to know who was responsible for Heinz's death if it wasn't an accident."

"If I come up with anything. Thanks for your help."

I hung up and took care of Eddie's immediate needs. Maybe it was time to call Joseph and sit down with her. My head was in a scramble and I couldn't see a way out. I grabbed a cookie for myself and went upstairs with Eddie.

Jack laughed when I described the phone call. "Sounds like he had a list of every fact you've written down so he could contradict it."

"You may be right. I went back and read my notes from this man Andrew Franklin in Minneapolis. He remembers helping Heinz down the stairs with his suitcases and putting him into an empty taxi that took off for the airport. Steve Millman says he and Heinz dragged their suitcases down the stairs and got in a taxi and went to the airport together. And they flew to Phoenix on the same plane."

"You know," my husband said reasonably, "it doesn't take much to put those two descriptions together if you're willing to forgive a man's twenty-year-old memory. Andrew Franklin helped Heinz downstairs and put him in an empty taxi. Then Franklin went back up to his room and studied for an exam. Steve Millman went down by himself a few minutes later and got in the taxi that Heinz was already in."

"They seemed so sure when they told me. Andrew Franklin swore no one else was in the taxi when it took off."

"Anyway, you've confirmed that Heinz went to Phoenix and stayed with Millman's family."

"Yes, but Steve added a rental car. And frankly, Jack, that's just not true. The police would have found it in the parking lot when they closed up the park at night."

"Unless someone else was with Heinz and that person drove it away and returned it. And paid for it."

"Someone else," I said.

"That's why the backpack was taken, to find the rental contract." He was using his hypothetical voice, the tone

175

that said, *This could have happened, but I'm not saying it did.*

"It gives me more unanswered questions. What if Heinz had the car keys in his pocket, which is where people usually keep them? The other person would've had a difficult time getting down to him to find them, not to mention getting back up. And he might have drawn attention to himself if people came by. Jack, this Marty McHugh, I keep thinking that he could have known all along where Steve Millman was, that he called the people I called just so that I would believe he was making the effort if I ever talked to them."

"You're starting to sound like me."

"You mean, *Trust no one?*"

"That sounds good. You know someone in that gang was with Heinz on the mountain. They're all telling you the same story: *I wasn't there.* The guy who's lying just blends in with the ones who're telling the truth. Somehow you've got to see what's different about his story, what points to him as a liar."

It was Steve whose story was different. The introduction of the rental car just didn't fit. I simply didn't believe it. And I didn't believe his father had made a firm commitment that Steve would appear at a job interview on the day of the scheduled hike. Both of those things sounded to me like rationalizations that had been worked out to explain away a painful truth.

"There's one person I believe in all this," I said. "Michael Borden. He didn't live on the corridor but he was Heinz's friend. Heinz told him he was going hiking with Steve Millman."

"And Millman confirms that Heinz came to the Millman house."

"Yes. But from that point, the stories diverge."

"Even so, you've got agreement now on where Heinz went after the semester was over and where Millman went, and you've put them together in the same house."

"And then the sun came up the next morning, on Cinco de Mayo," I said. "And nobody agrees on what happened after that."

I arranged for Elsie to pick up Eddie after school on Tuesday. I was going to the funeral and wasn't sure how long I would be away from home. When I reached Hillside Village, Dr. Farley took me aside.

"Would you be able to say a few words about Mrs. Gruner? It's a short service, and I'd like some friends to speak."

"Of course." I made a few notes in my notebook before I took my seat.

Before I entered the large room where the service was taking place, I noticed a man standing by himself against the wall in the corridor. He seemed to be watching the people who walked or rolled past him. I had the sense that he was aching for a cigarette.

Just on a chance, I walked over to him and said, "Mr. Koch?"

He looked startled. "Yes. Who are you?"

"Chris Bennett. We spoke on the phone yesterday. I'm glad you came. I hope we can talk."

177

"I'm busy this afternoon. I won't be going to the cemetery, but I can find some time, perhaps tomorrow." He pulled a small agenda out of his inside jacket pocket and flipped it open. "I have a free hour from eleven to twelve." He said it in a *take-it-or-leave-it* tone.

"I can be there. Give me the address."

He handed me a card, adding something in ink.

"I'll see you tomorrow." I went inside and sat down.

I was the third person called to speak. The other two were Dr. Farley and a woman who had known Mrs. Gruner for many years, having lived near her before she came to Hillside Village. I took my place at the lectern and talked about my long-ago acquaintanceship with Heinz Gruner and my new friendship with his mother. Ten minutes after I finished, the funeral was over.

I joined the residents who were riding to the cemetery in the bus. When the graveside service was over, I took the rose I had been given and laid it on top of the casket. This had been a brief and unexpected friendship for both of us, but one that each of us appreciated. I felt very sad that the life and the friendship had ended.

As the group moved back toward the bus, I stopped at Heinz's stone and said a prayer. Then I left a bunch of spring flowers I'd brought with me.

During lunch at Hillside Village, Dr. Farley asked if I was free to go to the bank with him. I said I was.

We left before most of the residents had finished eating and walked out to his car. He drove several miles and turned into a parking lot next to a bank. We went in, and he identified himself satisfactorily. I gave him the key and the clerk presented him with the box. Together we went to a small room with a dim light, a shelf, and one chair. He opened the box and started removing one paper after another. The top sheet was an inventory; as he came upon each item, he checked it off.

"This is her will," he said, extracting a thick envelope with a lawyer's return address. "I have a copy."

"Did she designate beneficiaries?"

"Most of it is going to the Rimson College Library. She and her late husband established an endowment to buy books in memory of their son. This will increase the principal so the college can buy more books each year."

"That's a good thing to do with the money," I said.

There was an insurance policy that dated from decades back. The beneficiary had become the Rimson College Library. A few government bonds were there, a mortgage application for a house she had not lived in for almost twenty years, some small family photographs, a few pieces of jewelry. A woman's diamond watch, a man's wedding ring, a bracelet in three colors of gold, and a couple of rings were wrapped in soft cotton cloth.

I found myself feeling sadder looking at the contents of the box than I had at the funeral and later at the cemetery.

"Are you all right?" Dr. Farley asked.

I shook my head.

He pulled out the chair and told me to sit. I followed

his suggestion, taking a tissue from my bag and drying my eyes.

"I understand," he said. "A life in a small box." He picked up the bracelet and looked at it, then the rings, which were gold and appeared to be quite old. "I'd like you to take one of these for yourself, Mrs. Brooks. I think Hilda would have been pleased to know you were wearing something from her family."

"What are you supposed to do with it?" I asked.

"Sell it and turn the proceeds over to the Rimson Library. There are no descendants, no immediate family."

"I think it should all go to the library."

He rewrapped the jewelry and put everything in the slim leather zipper case he was carrying. I pushed the chair back and stood, aware of the tightness of the space. Dr. Farley opened the door and settled with the clerk, closing the account on the box. When we opened the door to the bank, I was surprised by the brilliance of the sunshine.

18

I drove into New York the next morning and up to the Columbia University campus, the center of which is at West 116th Street. It's an impossible place to park at the best of times, but I drove around the streets for ten or fifteen minutes, hoping someone would abandon a meter or a legal spot on Riverside Drive where it costs nothing to park. No luck. I then drove to the only garage I knew of nearby and dropped off the car. Parking fees in New York are enough to cow the most sophisticated drivers, but Jack keeps telling me that when there's no alternative, swallow hard and pay the bill.

I walked back to the campus and found the building where Alfred Koch had his office. It was on the second floor; I walked up rather than wait for a creaky elevator. The building must have dated back to the days before World War II. Offices had wooden doors with large frosted-glass panes on the top half with numbers and professors' names painted in black, or no names at all.

Almost no one was about, the semester having just ended. But an occasional young person scooted by me, a cell phone at his ear. We have become a society that cannot stop talking. I knocked at Professor Koch's door and a voice called, "Enter."

It was a one-man office, two walls of books, one wall with a window overlooking the campus, and on the fourth wall books piled everywhere but the door.

"Please come in," Koch said, rising from behind a stacked desk. He held out his hand and we shook. "I have till noon. What did you want to talk about?"

"Your name came up in a letter Heinz Gruner wrote to his parents during the last semester he was at Rimson College. And I found a letter from you among the papers in Mrs. Gruner's room at Hillside Village. When I asked her about you, she became very upset."

He nodded sagely. "Yes, I can believe that. I was both welcome and unwelcome to the Gruner family. Ultimately, I was more of the former."

I waited for an explanation, but he was silent. "What was your role, Professor Koch?"

"I'm not sure I should disclose it to you. With the Gruners gone, that's a closed chapter. I see no reason to reopen it."

"That's what I'm here for, sir, to find out what was going on."

He contemplated a stack of files on his desk. "Let's just say I was instrumental in getting Heinz into Rimson College."

That surprised me. "Heinz was very bright. I wouldn't think he needed help."

"You're correct that he was very bright. And he tested well. There were extenuating circumstances in his case, and I was able to mediate a solution."

It sounded like gobbledygook to me. "You used to teach at Rimson," I said.

"That's right."

"Were you still teaching there at the time Heinz applied?"

He looked at the ceiling. "I believe I was negotiating with Columbia around that time, getting ready to leave Rimson and come to New York."

"Were you and the Gruners friends?"

"From a long time ago. We emigrated to the United States at different times, but we remained in touch."

"I'd like to know what the extenuating circumstances you referred to were."

"They had nothing to do with Heinz's death. I believe

182

that's what you're looking into."

"It is, and the facts of his death have developed into a much more complicated situation than anyone believed at first."

"Would you like to tell me how?"

I hated to give up what I knew with nothing promised in return, but I thought I might learn something if I did. "He wasn't alone when he died on that mountain."

"How could you possibly know that?" he said, sounding almost angry.

"I was in Arizona a few weeks ago, and I met the people who found his body and reported it to the police."

"And?"

I had the feeling I would not like to be a student in one of his classes. If I responded incompletely or incorrectly, he might pounce on me, at least verbally. "And I have uncovered information that strongly indicates someone was with him."

"I can't see how you could determine that after so many years."

"Are you aware that one of Heinz's suitcases was sent to the Gruners weeks after he died?"

"I would assume the police did that."

"The police never found any suitcase belonging to Heinz. I spoke to the officer who was first on the scene after the report of a body being sighted. Heinz had two suitcases. Only one was sent to the Gruners; the other disappeared. He took both of them to Phoenix. There was no return name or address on the suitcase the

Gruners received. Someone assumed possession of both suitcases, took what he wanted from them, and sent only one back." I heard my voice almost mimicking his, becoming sterner in response to his scorn.

"What motivated you to investigate this tragedy so many years after it happened?"

"I knew him in high school. He was a nice person. I was invited to Arizona and my friend and I visited Picacho Peak. I have learned a great deal about what happened that day and I'm determined to continue. Someone was with Heinz, almost certainly a young man from Rimson, someone who lived on his corridor that semester. I've spoken to all of them, by the way."

"All of them?" he asked, sounding so skeptical it led me to believe that he knew that one of those young men had engineered a successful disappearance. But how could he possibly know that?

"Yes," I said innocently. "I've spoken to all of them. And Dean Hershey besides. He put me in touch with most of them."

He looked at me with piercing brown eyes. "Could you give me their names?"

"I don't have them with me." I was starting to enjoy his discomfort. Somehow he knew that Steve Millman could not be traced, but he didn't want to admit that to me. "Of course, none of them will say he was with Heinz at the time of the accident."

"Because Heinz was alone," Koch said, as though dismissing the whole topic.

"Heinz was not alone. One of those students on his

corridor was with him. I've been paring down the list. I'll have the right man soon."

"Well," he said with a smile, "let me know when you find out."

"I'd still like to know what part you played in Heinz's life."

"And I still consider that privileged." He looked at his watch. "Are we through here?"

"Yes, sir." I laid a piece of paper with my full name, address, and phone number on his desk. "If you change your mind and decide to cooperate, I'd like to hear from you."

"Mrs. Brooks, I have not been uncooperative. What I know cannot possibly help you. And I think there are reasonable explanations for your information that do not include putting another person from Rimson on that mountain. Think about it."

At that moment, his phone rang. He picked it up, listened, and said, "Robert, yes, I've been waiting to hear from you." He looked in my direction and waved.

I left.

I thought about our conversation as I drove home to Oakwood. I didn't like this man, but I was convinced he knew something relevant. His obvious surprise that I had spoken to everyone had set off an alarm. He knew that one member of that corridor could not be found using ordinary methods. Koch was too clever to give away the name of the missing man, and I wasn't going to unless I could get something important in return.

What I could not figure out was what part Koch had played in getting Heinz into Rimson. I had left high school halfway through the four-year curriculum, so I had no memory of junior and senior years. Had Heinz become ill and missed enough school that his finals were poor? Perhaps Maddie would remember. She would be my next call.

Late in the afternoon I called Maddie and we arranged to have lunch the next day about halfway between her town and mine. She knew a good restaurant and said she would make a reservation for noon.

It was evening when I realized that I had not heard from Herb Fallon for a few days. Nor had I thought to call him. He had been so eager to hear news last week that I wondered what had made his enthusiasm wane. After Jack and I had had our coffee in the evening, I called him at home.

"Chris, how's it going?" He sounded his usual ebullient self.

"Better than I expected. I talked to Steve Millman yesterday afternoon." Silence. "Herb?"

"Did you say what I think you said?"

"Steve Millman. We talked on the phone."

"How in hell did you manage that? His *mother* said she didn't know where he was."

"I expect his mother was protecting him. Marty McHugh found him."

"Amazing. So where is he?"

"I have no idea." I explained how we had been conferenced on Marty's phone.

"So Marty knows where he is."

"I guess so. He found him."

"This is—this is amazing. Nobody's seen the guy for twenty years and in a couple of days you found him."

"I think Marty knew where to look, Herb. I know he made a lot of calls."

"So what did he say?"

"He admitted that Heinz went to Arizona with him, that he stayed at the Millmans', but Steve insists he never went hiking with Heinz."

"Did he say who did go?"

"He claims not to know. He said Heinz rented a car to get to Picacho Peak. I don't believe it. I believe Steve was there and that they drove together in Steve's car, but I couldn't get Steve to change his story, and I don't know where he is or how to reach him. For all I know, after that phone call he may have picked himself up and moved again."

"Not likely," Herb said. "He's got to have a job now. You can't just walk out of a job and hope to land another good one. And he might have a family, kids in school. Marty must be a good friend, a trusted friend. He probably had a long talk with Steve before your conversation with a lot of promises made."

I had thought as much myself. "Well, I did the best I could. I've established that he's alive, and if he can be believed, he went to Arizona on the same plane as Heinz. Which makes Andrew Franklin's story some-what specious."

"It's a long time ago. Memories fade. I wouldn't hold it against Andy."

I smiled. The old friendships were still in place. "Well, I wanted to update you. And I don't think you know that Heinz's mother died over the weekend."

He said some appropriate words, and we concluded our conversation. It left me with a few uncomfortable questions that I hoped I would find answers to. Something made me think I had turned a corner in this case. I just didn't recognize the street I was now on.

19

In the morning I sat down with my lists again. The information I had was full of contradictions. Heinz was the only one in the taxi. Steve Millman rode to the airport in the some taxi as Heinz. Heinz rented a car to drive from Phoenix to Picacho Peak, but there was no record of any car having been found. Heinz was alone on his hike; someone was with Heinz on the trail. Heinz had two suitcases; only one suitcase was returned to the Gruners. The small backpack was not on the trail when the Towers went up the trail; the small backpack was at the side of the trail when the Towers came down.

I picked up the phone and called Andrew Franklin in Minneapolis. He had told me that Heinz was the only passenger in the taxi. When he answered, I reminded him who I was and told him I was rechecking information.

"OK," he said graciously. "What can I tell you today?"

"You said you helped Heinz Gruner down the dorm stairs to a taxi."

"That's right. He had two suitcases. I took one."

"Where did those suitcases go in the taxi?"

"Into the trunk."

"Were there any other suitcases in that trunk?"

"No. Just his."

"What happened after the trunk was closed and Heinz was in the car?"

"They took off."

"And you think Heinz was alone in that taxi."

"I know he was. What's the problem?"

"I've been told that Steve Millman was in the taxi with Heinz."

"Steve Millman? I would remember that."

"Why would you remember that in particular?" I asked.

"Because he dropped out of school. I never saw him again after that semester. He was the guy who lived in Phoenix. I would surely remember if he flew to Arizona with Heinz. Heinz died on that trip. I never saw him again, either."

There wasn't much logic in what he was telling me, but he sounded as though he were explaining the facts to his satisfaction.

"Would it surprise you to know that I talked to Steve Millman this week and he said he was in that taxi?"

"Well, he should know," Andrew Franklin said

189

without a pause. "How is he? I haven't seen him for twenty years."

"He sounds fine," I said.

"Then who knows? Maybe my memory is playing tricks on me. Was there anything else?"

"Not at the moment. Thank you for your time."

He hadn't sounded flustered or annoyed, and he hadn't asked how I had located Steve Millman. Just a faulty memory and a bit of haste to get off the phone. Certainly there was no indication that Franklin was deliberately lying.

Besides Franklin, no one on the corridor had had such specific information. Either he was wrong or Steve Millman was lying. It was much easier to believe that Franklin's information was incorrect. Steve had done himself no favor by admitting that he had traveled with Heinz and that Heinz had stayed at the Millman home. I believed him. He had nothing to gain by admitting this if it weren't true. In fact, it made him look worse. I couldn't figure out why he would say what I had heard him say.

In the years since I was released from my vows at St. Stephen's, I have done more than become a secular person. I have developed a necessarily skeptical outlook. People lie. People adjust the truth to make themselves or their situation appear more positive. People hurt each other both spiritually and physically. It is impossible to believe everything you are told. As I sat reflecting on this strange case with its even stranger cast of characters, I began to wonder if I had spoken to

190

Steve Millman at all. Maybe Marty McHugh, for his own reasons, had enlisted a friend to play the part of Steve Millman. For all I knew, it might be someone who worked in the same company, who might even share an office with him. I picked up the phone and dialed Marty's number. He answered quickly.

"Marty," I said, "what assurance can you give me that the person I spoke to on Monday was actually Steve Millman?"

"I know it was Steve. I tracked him down and when I called him, I recognized his voice."

"I don't want to sound as though I doubt you, but—"

"But you doubt me."

"I would like to talk to him again—without you on the line—so that I can determine for myself that he is who he says he is."

"I don't see—"

"There are ways," I said. "He can call with one of those telephone cards that disguises where the call is coming from."

"Right. My wife keeps one in her purse when she doesn't carry her cell. Look, I'll call him and see what he says. What's your problem with having me on the line?"

"Maybe he'll be more forthcoming if it's a private conversation."

"Yeah, right. OK, I'll get back to you."

My concern was that if Steve said something Marty didn't want me to know, Marty could sever the connection. Or if the person playing the part of Steve was in

Marty's office and I asked a question, Marty could scribble the answer and shove it over to him. Goodness, I thought, I had certainly become a doubter.

Just before twelve I called Mrs. Millman. She answered on the second ring, and I told her that I wanted to ask her some questions about the summer Steve came home from Rimson with a friend.

"What friend?" she said.

"He had a German-sounding name, Heinz Gruner."

"I don't remember that."

"It was the last semester that Steve was at Rimson. I heard he flew to Phoenix with Heinz and Heinz stayed overnight."

"With us?"

"Yes, at your house."

"I'm not sure. I have two other children and some-times the house was full of guests. I couldn't say if this boy came home with Steve and if it was when you said."

"He and Steve were going to go hiking at Picacho Peak."

"That's down near Tucson," Mrs. Millman said.

"Yes. They were going to climb up one of the trails."

"It's such a long time ago. I can't really say."

"Did you talk to Professor Fallon last week?"

"Professor who?"

"Fallon. Herb Fallon. He was an old friend of Steve's from Rimson College."

She didn't answer.

"I think he called you in the middle of last week," I said.

"I don't remember that at all."

I started wondering if her memory was failing. I could understand not recalling an overnight guest twenty years ago, but a phone call last week from her son's old college friend should have made an impression. "He was trying to reach Steve. He asked you for Steve's phone number."

"I don't give that out. Steve doesn't like to get phone calls."

"Well, thank you for your help," I said, giving up.

"It's no trouble," the voice replied.

That threw me for a loop. Had she forgotten or had Herb lied to me? He knew I had her phone number and might call her, so if he concocted the story of the phone call, he might easily be found out. But at this point in my investigation, I no longer had a sense of who was telling me the truth and who wasn't.

I picked up the phone again and called St. Stephen's. An unfamiliar voice answered and I asked for Sister Joseph. When Joseph came on, I told her I was not only not getting to the heart of the case, but on the verge of becoming paranoid as well.

Her laugh told me how preposterous she thought my statement was. "It sounds as though you're ready for a visit."

"I am indeed. If you're available tomorrow, I can manage it."

"Come in time for lunch."

20

I was running late for my lunch with Maddie, so I dashed. She had suggested a diner that I vaguely remembered from my youth, a place that cooked large, tasty dishes. It was frequented by hometown adults for lunch and dinner and by high school kids in the evening, especially after the local movie finished.

Maddie was already in a comfortable booth and she grinned and waved as I came in, then slid off the bench to hug me. I apologized for being a few minutes late and grabbed the menu, which was so large, I felt daunted.

"They have good luncheon specials," Maddie said, directing me to a section that had several choices that suited me. As I glanced down the list, we exchanged family gossip. I waited till our orders had been taken before broaching the subject that had brought us together.

"I've been thinking about Heinz since you called," she said. "I never saw him again after we graduated. He went off to some college in the Midwest and I went to Ithaca College for two years. So I didn't see him the last couple of years of his life."

"Think back, Maddie. Think back to your last two years in high school. Did anything happen to him? Was there any gossip about him?"

"Gossip? About Heinz Gruner? There was nothing to gossip about. I don't think he dated, at least not anyone

194

I knew. He studied, he played an instrument, but I don't remember which one. He was always in the honors classes. I'm not being helpful, am I?"

"Let's keep going. Did you remember to bring the yearbook?"

"Right here." She handed it across the table.

I opened it and flicked to the page where Heinz's graduation picture appeared. He was smiling and his dark hair was unkempt. I smiled too and read the few lines below the photo. It mentioned his achievements briefly, his interests, and at the bottom said he was going to attend Harvard University.

"That's interesting," I said aloud. "Heinz was expecting to go to Harvard when the yearbook was printed."

"But he didn't. He went to Rimson College in Illinois."

"Maybe his grades weren't good enough for Harvard."

"Possibly."

I flipped some pages and found the history club. There was Heinz in the first row. Near him were several boys and girls I remembered from my two years in the school. He wasn't in the science club or the math club but he was in the chess club and the English club. Obviously his talents were centered in the arts.

"Did anyone in our class go to Harvard that year?" I asked.

"I don't think so. Paul Garner went to Princeton and Eric Wallace went to Yale. There may have been others."

Heinz's name and photo did not appear in any sports groups, but he'd apparently acted in several school plays. Why had he written Harvard down if he didn't go there? And was Alfred Koch involved in his choice?

"Maybe Harvard was his first choice," I said, "and Rimson was his safe school."

"Rimson wasn't exactly the kind of school that kids thought was safe. It was a tough school to get into."

"But maybe not as tough as Harvard."

"Why does it matter?" Maddie asked.

"I don't know that it does. I'm just trying to clear up questions that have come up. Nothing fits, Maddie. Something very strange went on in the last days of Heinz's life. People I've spoken to have lied to me and—"

"Why would they do that, and how do you know they did?"

"I know because I get different answers to the same question. And they have to be doing it to protect someone, but I'm not sure who or why they would do that. It's very confusing."

"I can see that. It's as if you have no anchor to hang on to."

"That's just what it feels like." I finished turning the pages of the yearbook and handed it back to her. "Do you know who his friends were in high school?"

"One guy." She opened the yearbook and turned to the photos. She looked intently at the pictures. "Here he is, Don Shiller."

"I remember him," I said. "Not too tall, good in math."

"That's the one. He and Heinz always ate together in the cafeteria."

I looked back through the years, recalling the cafeteria with its long tables and horrible food, and saw the two boys sitting opposite each other, eating and talking. I had taken algebra with Don, and he had seemed to catch on to everything while I was slow to grasp what it was all about.

"Do you know what happened to him?"

"I don't think I ever saw him again," Maddie said. "But his folks still live in town. They're in the phone book."

"Good. That's someone out of the Rimson circle. At least he won't be influenced by the students on Heinz's corridor."

"You are something, Chris," Maddie said. "You really think you'll figure out what happened all those years ago?"

"I'm a lot closer than I was when I started. I just need to hit the right person or get some new piece of information that will make sense of all the little pieces I've assembled."

"Well, good luck."

That was what I needed, I thought.

At home I found the Shiller listing and called it. Don's mother answered. She didn't remember me—I hadn't thought she would—but she gave me her son's home phone number. He was teaching mathematics at a college in Pennsylvania and was generally home in the evening. I hung up feeling almost relieved that I could spend the rest of the afternoon away from the Heinz Gruner case.

I reached him after dinner. He actually remembered me from my two years in his high school. We reminisced for a few minutes and then I turned the discussion to Heinz.

"Heinz," he said, and his voice changed. "He was my best friend. I was destroyed when he died."

I explained my interest in Heinz's death, and he said he would do anything he could to help. I asked if he knew that Heinz intended to go to Arizona to hike in the mountains.

"He wrote to me in the spring of that year. He said his parents were giving him a trip to Arizona as a birthday present. He asked if I could come, but I couldn't. I don't think there was any special reason, just that money was tight in my family and I had a job waiting for me when the school year was over. I wish I had gone. He'd be alive today."

"Why do you say that?"

"From what I heard, he fell from one of the trails. I'm sure I could have prevented that. We knew each other well. We got along. If he wasn't feeling well or the heat got to him, he would have told me. His death was the greatest tragedy of my life."

"Don, I don't think Heinz died in an accidental fall."

"What are you saying?"

I explained. He listened carefully, then said. "That's incredible. I've always thought he just got sunstroke and collapsed. You're telling me someone murdered him?"

"That's not what I'm saying. I'm saying someone was with him. Whatever happened on that trail, the other person didn't report Heinz's fall. That person also took Heinz's two suitcases, probably rifled through them, and sent one back to his parents."

"No return address."

"Right. So what I want to know from you is, did he tell you who was going to Arizona with him?"

"Can I call you back tomorrow night on that? I actually saved some of his letters and I can put my hands on them. And I'd like to give all of this some thought."

I gave him my number. "I'll be here tomorrow night."

21

The next morning I drove north at a leisurely pace in order to enjoy the scenery, especially my glimpses of the Hudson River. It was a fine day. Elsie had agreed to pick Eddie up from school, so my time wasn't limited. I arrived about eleven thirty and stopped first at the Villa to see the retired nuns. A couple of them had begun to show their age, not only in their looks but also in an unaccustomed lack of energy, in aches and pains that forced them to move more slowly, to pause in their meanderings.

When we had all exchanged our bits of news, I walked over to the Mother House and went up the stone steps to where Joseph's office was. I knocked, heard her voice, and stepped inside.

"Chris, how good to see you." She stood from her desk chair and came to hug me. "You look wonderful. Have you persuaded Jack to give up the East Coast and buy a house in Arizona?"

I laughed. "Jack is one of those people who hardly believes there's life west of the Hudson. But I think he may agree to a visit some winter. I don't know how many generations of his family have lived in New York. That means a lot to him. Is anything happening with the convent?" She would know that I was asking about its future.

"Nothing has changed. We're still talking and thinking and weighing options. Let's go down to lunch. We'll do our talking when we come up."

Whenever I return for a visit, I shake a lot of hands and answer a lot of questions. Often Joseph and I eat off trays in her office. I was happy this time to have the chance to see all the faces at all the tables. But it was hard not to notice that the number of tables had decreased. A few of the middle-aged nuns had left; a few of the older ones had died. That was the problem, and I had come to accept that the situation would never be reversed.

We had a tasty and pleasurable lunch. As always, a bag of homemade cookies was presented to me to take home to my family. I would have two happy faces at the dinner table that night.

When the lunch and the small talk were over, Joseph and I went back upstairs and sat in our usual places opposite each other at the long table. I had all the paperwork I had collected from the case, and I placed it on the table where we could refer to it. The early parts of the mystery were known to Joseph, of course, as she had been right there with me in Arizona.

"Why don't you start with what happened after we returned from our glorious trip?" she said.

That was easy enough. I began with my conversation with Dean Hershey, who had overnighted the list of students' names, and continued with my calls, especially the one to Prof. Herb Fallon. She agreed as I talked that it was difficult to imagine that these men could remember who had left first at the end of the semester, who had gone where, who had traveled alone, and who had gone solo. I observed her listing the names and making notes next to them.

I included my visits to Mrs. Gruner, her helpfulness until the moment I found the letter from Alfred Koch, and her subsequent death and burial.

"Have you had an opportunity to talk to Mr. Koch?" Joseph asked.

"I saw him Wednesday," I said, recounting the unsatisfying meeting in his office at Columbia.

"Why do you think he's hiding anything relevant?"

"I suppose because I think many people are hiding relevant information. Heinz is dead. His parents are dead. I'm clearly not going to broadcast whatever his secret is to the world. Who would care?"

"It may not be clear to him. And perhaps it's what Mr. Koch did, not what Heinz Gruner did, that he wants to keep secret."

I considered that. Possibilities flew through my mind. He had had Heinz's SATs altered. He had bribed someone to eliminate a police report. He had coerced a teacher to write a better recommendation to Rimson. I'm starting to think like a cop, I thought.

"I hadn't thought of that" was all I said.

She told me to go on and I finished the story, including my phone call to Don Shiller and what might be the most important event of all, the discovery of Steve Millman and my conversation with him.

"Why couldn't he call you himself?" Joseph asked.

"The excuse was that it's easy to get the number of a caller, but it's not a good excuse."

"And Mr. McHugh monitors everything both of you say."

"Yes." I then told her that I had requested a call without Marty on the line.

"I doubt whether he'll do it," Joseph said. "Under the guise of keeping Mr. Millman's location secret, Mr. McHugh was able to hear the entire conversation."

"Why would he want to do that?" I asked, knowing that I, too, had considered this possibility. "If Steve killed Heinz, whether by design or by accident, what difference would that make to Marty McHugh?"

"Maybe Mr. McHugh was a third man on the mountain and doesn't want to be implicated in Heinz Gruner's death."

I leaned back to consider this. "Steve Millman was responsible for Heinz Gruner's death and Marty McHugh saw what happened and didn't report it to the authorities. So we have a conspiracy of silence. I still don't see what Marty is worried about. Steve is hardly going to tell me the truth about what happened. He'll be in much worse trouble than Marty."

"I think 'conspiracy' is the important word in all this. We may not yet know everything that happened on the trail, Chris."

"Let's go back to what you said a minute ago, that Marty McHugh was a third man on the mountain. You know, that could explain a couple of things, Joseph. Maybe Heinz did get into an empty taxi, because Marty and Steve had left earlier in their own taxi. The other thing is, when I met Marty, he said he'd never been to Arizona but he didn't like it; it had too much blue sky and dry heat and you had to carry water with you so you wouldn't dehydrate. He was talking about when he was there."

"I think you're right, Chris. He slipped up. And if he and Steve took a taxi together, it means that the man from Minneapolis told you the truth. It was Steve, the possible killer, and Mr. McHugh who lied to cover each other."

The conspiracy, I thought. "Then that would mean that two young men were guests at the Millmans' that night. And all three of them drove to Picacho Peak the next day. And Marty McHugh, who was apparently the most helpful person I spoke to, and who treated me to an extravagant lunch, has turned out to be the biggest liar." My frustration was audible.

"Don't make any firm determinations about who has lied and who has told you the truth. All we're doing here is tossing around some hypotheses. But I agree with you that Mr. McHugh's insistence on being on the line with Steve Millman is cause for suspicion."

I nodded, still not sure.

"Let's take a look at the professor you've been speaking to, the historian from Rimson."

"Herb Fallon. He was very helpful and enthusiastic when we began to talk, but he hasn't gotten back to me lately." I told her I had called him myself two days before, and he had been surprised that I'd spoken to Steve Millman. "Also," I said, "his report of what Mrs. Millman told him differs from what she told me. She told him she didn't know if she could reach her son."

"She *allegedly* told him," Joseph corrected me.

"He really went out of his way for me, Joseph. He checked up on alumni who had never changed their addresses with the college, gave me addresses I didn't have. He found Marty McHugh for me."

"Let's keep that in mind."

"You're becoming as skeptical as my husband."

"Your husband is in a business that requires healthy skepticism. And you've said yourself, one or more of these men have lied to you. You have to be careful what you say to them until you know which category each one belongs to."

"I'm afraid you're right. I'm going to talk to an old high school friend of Heinz's tonight. He's not part of the Rimson crowd, so perhaps he's more believable."

"I think you're going to figure this out, Chris. The fact that Steve Millman actually agreed to talk to you is very encouraging. But you're right, there is clearly a conspiracy here. We don't know how many men are part of it or what their motives are, but they want to keep you and the law from finding out what happened on that trail."

"I agree. I just can't figure out why anyone would want to hurt Heinz Gruner."

"Maybe they didn't, Chris."

I looked at her, but her face showed nothing. That was her message to me.

I stopped at Elsie's house and picked up Eddie, staying for a cup of tea before we went home. Elsie has enabled me to have a life outside of motherhood without worry. She's as good as a grandmother, and Eddie is still happy to visit her. I suppose that will change one day, but I try not to think about it. On this day he was especially happy, carrying a bag of Elsie's cookies out to the car and discovering that a second bag awaited him.

"Did Sister Dolores make these for me?"

"She sure did, but she made them for Daddy, too, so don't go eating them all up."

"I think Daddy is too old to eat cookies," my son said.

I laughed. "Eddie, that's a terrible thing to say."

"Then why are you laughing?"

"Good question. Because what you said tickled me. Just remember, no man is ever too old for cookies."

"OK. Can I try just one now?"

"Sure. Please don't get crumbs in the car."

"I'll be careful." He opened the bag and pulled out a cookie fit for a king. It was gone by the time we turned into the driveway.

22

Don Shiller called before I brewed our after-dinner coffee. "I found Heinz's letters," he said, "and some of them seem relevant to what you want to know. Here's one." He quoted from the letter:

> My parents have decided to give me a trip as a birthday present. I think they expected me to go to Europe but I'm not ready for that. I've always wanted to hike in the Southwest and if I can manage, I can be out of here on May fourth and on some great trail on the fifth—which, I'm sure you remember, is Cinco de Mayo: the day General Zaragoza was victorious at the battle of Puebla in 1862 after the execution of Maximilian. Imagine, we might have had a French country south of the border.

"I have another one," Don went on, and I heard him unfolding paper.

> One of the guys on my corridor lives in Phoenix and he says I can stay at his house while I'm hiking. He doesn't have his own car but his parents can double up while I'm there and we'll use his mother's. He says it's only about an hour's drive to Picacho Peak, which is on the way to Tucson and a good place to hike. I'm getting pretty excited about this. I wish you were joining me.

"He goes on to talk about a course he's taking. There's one more."

> A really crazy coincidence. This guy from Phoenix has something like a family connection to me. He doesn't know it, but I realized it from something he said. He's a weird guy but I don't want to bore you.

"Don," I said, "could you read that again about the family connection?"

He located it and read it slowly while I took down as much of it as I could manage. "Is that it? He doesn't elaborate anywhere on that family business?"

"No. I read through all the letters—there aren't many—and that's all he says about that. I never found out any more about it."

I let it go for the moment. "And that's it?"

"I'm afraid so. The one I just read you is the last letter he ever wrote me."

"Don, does he mention the name Alfred Koch in any of the letters?"

"No. He doesn't mention many names at all. It's usually this guy and that guy. The only name he ever mentions is someone he refers to as 'my friend Herb Fallon.'"

"I've spoken to him several times and I did have the feeling that they were friends. But Herb says he didn't hear about Heinz's death until sometime in the summer. When did you hear?"

"Maybe a week after it happened. I was still away at school—Rimson let out early—and my mother called me. I knew when I heard her voice that something terrible had happened. She didn't approve of long-distance calls. She said there was a notice in the local paper and she had called Mrs. Gruner. She went to the funeral. I couldn't leave school. It was finals time." He still felt bad about that. His voice was full of remorse.

"There was nothing you could do," I said, hoping to give him small comfort. "So besides Herb Fallon, no one else's name is mentioned?"

"Not that I saw. I'll read the letters over later and if I find any names, I'll call you. He never even mentions the name of this guy who lived in Phoenix."

"What I'm wondering is whether he says anywhere that anyone else was going to Arizona besides the guy from Phoenix?"

"I don't think so, but I'll keep my eye open for a name."

"Thank you, Don. You've really been very helpful."

I made the coffee when I got off the phone. Jack came into the kitchen, eyeing the plate of cookies and giving me a sly smile. "I heard the end of your conversation. You think there was another person on that hike?"

"Joseph suggested it, and it answers some questions. This man Marty McHugh—"

"Who took you to an expensive lunch."

I grinned at him. "One and the same. He was on the line when I talked to Steve Millman the other day. Joseph's theory—or hypothesis—is that McHugh went along for the hike and saw what happened, but didn't report it. I've asked him if I can talk to Steve without him on the line. I haven't heard back."

"You won't."

"Because he has something to gain by hearing the conversation. Or something to lose by not hearing it. Joseph suggested that Steve Millman may have been instrumental in Heinz's death, and Martin McHugh may have seen what happened."

"And wants to keep his involvement a secret. It's a good theory."

"It also explains an inconsistency." I told him about the man who swore he had put Heinz in an empty taxi and watched him drive away, while Steve claimed to have been in the taxi and gone to the airport with Heinz.

"So Steve is lying to cover up the fact that McHugh went to Arizona."

"And that's why Marty wants to be on the line when I talk to Steve."

"You have any reason to believe they killed Heinz?"

"Jack, I don't know why anyone would kill Heinz. I just talked to his oldest friend from high school, Don Shiller. He read me parts of three letters that Heinz wrote to him in the last months of his life. It's all so innocent. Heinz talks about wanting to be there to hike on Cinco de Mayo. He says he's going with this guy who lives in Phoenix."

"That's Millman."

"That's Millman. And then he says something odd: that this guy—he never mentions the name—is kind of related to him."

"Interesting."

The coffee had made its way into the carafe, and Jack removed the grounds. I took the cookies into the family room and he followed me with the coffee.

"And that's it, no follow-up. Oh yes, he mentions that the Millmans have two cars and they'll let Heinz and his friend use one to drive to Picacho Peak."

"So no talk about renting."

"No. I'm afraid most of what Steve Millman told me was untrue, except for the fact that Heinz stayed overnight with the Millmans."

"So how's my friend Sister Joseph?" he said, switching to a happier subject.

"She's fine. Nothing's new with the convent. Dolores baked for you and Eddie."

"Then I don't have to share with you?" He looked

pixieish, very much like his son.

"Two of a kind," I said. "Eddie thought you were too old to eat cookies."

"My kid said that about me?"

"As he dug into Dolores's bag."

"Boy. I never would've thought."

At nine on Friday morning I called Marty McHugh. "Any progress on getting me a private chat with Steve Millman?" I asked.

"He just won't go for it," Marty said. "I'm sorry. It's out of the question."

"I talked to another old friend of Heinz's yesterday," I said, "and he confirmed that Heinz went hiking with Steve." I waited for his response.

"Who was this person?" Marty asked finally.

"A high school friend. You wouldn't know him, but I knew him."

"He must have heard that before Heinz's trip, because Steve says he didn't go on the hike."

"Right," I said, as though he had just reminded me of that "fact." "I forgot Steve didn't go. Or says he didn't go."

"Why would he lie about it?" Marty said.

"Because whoever was with Heinz knows the truth about what happened."

"You still think someone was with him."

"I *know* someone was with him."

"Well, if you figure out who it was, I'd like to know."

"And if Steve decides to come around and talk to me one-on-one, I'm available."

"I'll keep that in mind."

I'm sure you will, I thought as I hung up. I was convinced that he had never called Steve about a private conversation; he had just made the decision himself. Joseph was right. Marty McHugh was the third man on the mountain.

It now appeared that there were two possible events that may have happened on the trail on the mountain in Arizona. The first was that a terrible accident had occurred while the three young men were hiking. The two survivors had made a pact never to tell anyone lest it appear that one or both of them be considered responsible for Heinz's death. I could imagine that they were afraid to report the accident for fear of being implicated; or perhaps they were just young and scared and they gave in to their instinct to run and leave the tragedy behind.

The second possibility was that one of those young men had a grudge against Heinz for a reason I could not imagine. Or perhaps an argument developed as they hiked and Steve or Marty pushed Heinz, without meaning to take his life. It might have been a spur-of-the-moment thing, or involved the plagiarism, or perhaps the failure to repay a loan.

I admitted to myself that I was disappointed in Marty McHugh. I had felt so sorry for him after the plagiarism story that I didn't want to believe he was involved in

Heinz's death. I saw him as honorable and mistakenly tainted. Now I had to accept that he was part of a cover-up at the very least and that he had caused a death at the worst. Everything and everyone in this case had been turned upside down.

Finally I dialed Herb Fallon's office number. He didn't answer so I tried him at home. His wife answered and got him to the phone.

"Hiya, Chris. Got something?"

"More confusion," I said. "I don't know if you can help on this, but Marty McHugh told me last week when we had lunch that he had been accused of plagiarism, and it kept him from graduating with his class. Is there any way you could check on who the professor was, and what Marty allegedly did to earn that accusation?"

"Sounds more like arts than sciences. I'll check his classes and see if the professors are still around. This was almost twenty years ago, so I doubt he picked up anything off the Internet."

"He didn't. He said he was charged with copying someone's paper, or part of it, when in fact it was the other way around. He took a course over the summer and got his degree in the fall, but it's obvious he neither forgave nor forgot."

"What does this have to do with Heinz's death?"

"Probably nothing. I'm trying to get a handle on McHugh."

"I'll get right on it."

Since I had begun to doubt the veracity of everyone

on that corridor except the ones who could tell me nothing, I wondered whether Fallon would actually look into the alleged plagiarism. It had gone through my mind that if McHugh was lying about when the event took place, perhaps his gripe was with Heinz, and that could be my sought-after motive for murder. Marty had said the event had taken place in his last semester, which was why his graduation had been held up. At this point, I was skeptical of everything he had told me.

I did some necessary shopping, returning home in time for lunch and a look at the *Times*. Jack checked in, and I told him I had sent Herb on another mission.

"It's getting dangerous to talk to you," he said.

"I don't know where else to go," I admitted.

Nor did he.

Later in the day Herb called back.

"Got something for you," he said. "I went through the history and English professors on McHugh's transcript and called all the ones who are still here. The ones from his senior year claimed to know nothing about any plagiarism involving him. So I went back through the years and I actually found a lit professor from a course McHugh took in his sophomore year who said he remembered something."

I started feeling tingly. "McHugh was accused of plagiarism in his sophomore year?"

"Not exactly."

I laughed. "Herb, you're not making this easy for me."

"What I mean is, something happened. I talked to the

professor who taught the lit class Marty took, and he refused to tell me what it was all about. When I explained that you were looking into Heinz Gruner's death, he agreed to talk to you."

"That's sounding better."

Herb dictated the number and told me to call at five eastern time. The professor would speak to me from his office. I thanked Herb, feeling better about our relationship although I knew I had little reason to. As always, he promised to keep in touch.

After Eddie came home and had drunk his milk and eaten cookies, I checked with Jack and then called my friend Arnold Gold at his law office.

"Chrissy," he said jubilantly. "Haven't heard from you for a while. Looking for word processing work?"

"Not at the moment. I want to invite you both for Sunday afternoon. We haven't seen you for so long and the weather is lovely."

"Let me check out our busy schedule. Let's see, Sunday. Looks open to me. I'll say yes unless Harriet has something else on the calendar that I don't know about."

"Wonderful. Come anytime after twelve—the earlier, the better. The lieutenant will do the cooking so I promise you a great meal."

He laughed. "Haven't been disappointed yet. We'll see you Sunday."

I'd met Arnold while I was looking into a forty-year-old murder soon after I was released from my vows, and he, his wife, and I have become fast friends. That I married a cop who'd studied law only strengthened the bond.

I went outside, and Eddie and I weeded the garden. I did a little hoeing besides, turning over the brown earth that I love. The smell alone intoxicates me.

At five I went inside and dialed the number for Professor Addison at Rimson College. He answered on the first ring: "Addison."

"Professor Addison, this is Christine Bennett. I talked to Herb Fallon earlier today—"

"Yes, of course. He tells me you're looking into the untimely death of a onetime student here at Rimson."

I gave him a few details, listening to his periodic "uh-huhs" as I laid out the story.

"Well, that's quite interesting about Mr. McHugh. If he was charged with plagiarism in his senior year, it wasn't by me. He was in only one of my classes, English literature as I recall, and that was definitely not in his senior year. I had no part in his not graduating with his class, if that, in fact, is true."

"I don't know whether it's true," I said. "It's what he told me. I found the story of his alleged plagiarism quite moving and I felt sorry for him. He said that he eventually ran into the person from whom he was supposed to have lifted material—but that in fact it had happened in reverse—and got him to admit that he had stolen from Marty."

"I know nothing about that. It's possible that it's true. I did insist that Mr. McHugh take another English course to clear his name. He did that the following year."

216

"Professor Addision, I really need to know who the other party in this affair was."

"I'm not sure that I should divulge that, Ms. Bennett."

"Sir, I am trying to find out how Heinz Gruner died. I am quite sure that someone on his dorm corridor that year was responsible."

"Well, let me not shilly-shally. I checked my class records an hour ago—I keep all of them forever, to my wife's dismay—and I have the name."

I closed my eyes, waiting to hear him say *Heinz Gruner*.

"The person he plagiarized—or the other way around, if you will—was a young man named Steven Millman."

"Steve Millman," I echoed. "I must say that's a surprise."

"Surprise or not, that's who it was. Is there anything else I can tell you?"

I tried to think quickly. "Was Heinz Gruner ever a student of yours?"

"Not that year and, let me see, not the year before."

"Those are the only possible years," I said. "He died at the end of that semester."

"I do recall that."

"Well, thank you very much. You've been very helpful." I hung up feeling almost dizzy. My hope of finding a motive for the death of my old acquaintance had evaporated. What on earth had happened on that mountain almost twenty years before?

23

I took Saturday off from actively pursuing the case, although Jack and I talked about it when we had the opportunity. There were many preparations to be made for our guests and Jack and I discussed the menu, which I had to admit was more enjoyable than thinking about that unfortunate death.

Since it was warm, we decided to barbecue, and Jack said we should spring for filet mignon, which Prince's had on sale just for the weekend. The price still nearly knocked me off my feet but I grabbed a package and dashed down a nearby aisle before I had second thoughts.

At home we scrubbed the patio table and chairs till they gleamed, and then Jack did all the preparation that could be accomplished a day in advance so that he would have as little as possible to do when we returned from church on Sunday.

It was a hectic but relaxing day, at least for my over-worked mind. When we were finally alone in the evening, I told Jack about my conversation with Professor Addison the day before.

"Well, that's unexpected," he said. "Maybe they weren't after Heinz."

"I'm afraid Heinz may have been implicated in the plot, though."

"Sure puts a different face on things. But what points to his having a part in an attempted murder?"

"Just the fact that he wasn't the intended victim but he was there."

"You still haven't convinced me that this wasn't a terrible accident rather than a homicide. Three guys on a mountain, one of them slips and falls, two of them run like scared rabbits—"

"And drive away with Heinz's suitcases, which they loot."

"But then the crimes, if you want to call them that, are failure to report an accident and stealing. That doesn't add up to murder."

He was right, and I had no answer for him. Either something was missing or the ethics of those young men were well below what passed for normal—albeit somewhere above criminal.

I thought later in the evening of Don Shiller's quote that there was a family relationship between Steve and Heinz. That was still as puzzling to me as it had been when he read it to me from the letter. Enough, I thought. Think about tomorrow and your company.

Arnold and Harriet arrived at twelve thirty. We made ourselves comfortable in the family room, which was well cooled, and Harriet delivered a couple of small gifts to Eddie. One of them was a toy that a friend of his had just been given, and he jumped up and down to see it. After we had exchanged family information, Arnold asked us what we were up to. Jack glanced at me briefly and told our guests that I was looking into a twenty-year-old unexplained death, and we were off and running.

Arnold teased me, Harriet put him in his place and asked to hear all about it, and eventually I delivered an abbreviated sketch of my case.

"Nice," Arnold said, "three men on a mountain and one of them dies. Not a very strong motive, if you don't mind my saying so."

"I don't mind at all. Please shoot holes in anything I say. It may help me get to the right place. Nothing seems to be right at this moment."

"Who kills a guy for plagiarizing his work?"

"Allegedly, the victim paid for it, the plagiarizer didn't."

"It's still weak," Arnold said. "I'd get him off in ten minutes. I think something's missing."

"I do, too," I agreed. "I just don't know where to look for it."

"Well, I'm firing up the grill," Jack said. "No use going hungry while we talk."

We moved out-of-doors, taking our drinks with us. The patio table was out of the sun thanks to the umbrella, and we sat down and kept talking. I listened carefully to what everyone said. Two new points of view were present, and one of them might see something that I had missed.

"This Koch person," Arnold said at one point, "how does he fit into this thing?"

I explained Mrs. Gruner's violent reaction when I asked about Alfred Koch. "I've spoken to him, but I left feeling cheated. He didn't tell me much and he was—how can I describe it?—overbearing. There was one memorable moment in our conversation. I told him I had spoken to every man who had lived on that corridor and he said 'All of them?' or something like that, as though he didn't believe me."

"But you did," Harriet said.

"I definitely did, including Steve Millman, my main suspect. If it *was* Steve Millman I was talking to. I didn't place the call to him." I described the arrangement.

"So it could have been anyone," Arnold said.

"Yes. And it may have just been someone Marty McHugh picked out of a hat to do an acting job."

"You need to talk to him again and ask him some key questions," Harriet said. "But I don't know what those questions would be."

I had to admit I wasn't sure what they would be, either.

I got busy with serving our dinner then and we dropped the subject. Arnold got up and threw a ball to Eddie, who caught with his baseball mitt. They were a good pair. Eventually, Jack joined them and they formed a triangle while I kept my eye on that expensive beef.

The dinner was a great success. The meat was easily the best I had ever eaten, enhanced by Jack's surprise of a béarnaise sauce he had made while I wasn't looking. Eddie wasn't crazy about it but the rest of us were. We all overate and still had a good amount left over for another meal.

After a rest, I went inside and brewed some coffee,

taking out Aunt Meg's fine English bone china cups and saucers to serve it in. We had pastries from our favorite bakery, and I set everything up in the family room as the heat outside was becoming uncomfortable. Just as I was about to sit and enjoy my dessert, the phone rang. I dashed back to the kitchen, grabbed the receiver, and walked into the dining room so as not to disturb my guests.

"Miss Bennett, this is Alfred Koch."

"Professor Koch, yes."

"I've been thinking about our conversation of a few days ago. Did I hear you correctly when you said you had spoken to all the men who lived on Heinz Gruner's corridor the last semester of his life?"

"Yes, you did. I've done a lot of telephoning in the last couple of weeks, and I've been able to reach all of them."

"Could you read that list to me?"

"Just a moment." I put the phone down and rummaged for my list. "Here it is: Herb Fallon, Steven Millman, Barry Woodson, Andrew Franklin, Arthur Howell, Jereth Phillips, Eric Goode, and Martin McHugh."

"I see."

I waited. There was a long silence. Finally he said, "Perhaps we should speak again. Can you come to my office tomorrow morning?"

"I think I can make it."

"Eleven will be good for me."

I was just annoyed enough at his attitude that I said,

"I can't be there till eleven thirty."

"That will be satisfactory." He hung up.

I went back to the family room and reported the new turn of events.

"You've got him," Arnold said. "He can't believe you spoke to that fellow who's been hiding out all these years."

"And I can't prove I really talked to him. But this should be interesting. I knew he was holding something back. I hope he's ready to give it up."

"Don't believe everything you hear," my husband said, and everyone laughed.

The first thing I did on Monday morning was call Dean Hershey.

"Ah, Miss Bennett. I ran into Herb Fallon on campus the other day and we discussed your investigation. He's quite impressed with your progress."

"Thank you. I'm a bit surprised at it but I'm still not at a point where I can identify the person responsible for Heinz Gruner's death."

"It sounds as though that's just around the corner." His voice was almost jovial. "What can I do for you today?"

"I have a question or two about Prof. Alfred Koch." I gave him a moment to go back in time and place the name.

"Koch, yes. He used to teach history here, but he's been gone a long while. I think he was wooed away by Columbia."

223

"He was. I've met him a couple of times and I'm going to see him again later this morning, but I wanted to talk to you first. He had some connection to Heinz Gruner, a connection that distressed Heinz's mother when I last spoke to her. Do you have any idea what that might have been?"

"Let me see. That was a long time ago. What he did at Rimson, besides teaching history, was his job as a scout. He had connections with high schools in various places around the country, good high schools that produced the kind of candidates we were looking for. We're a small school, you know. We try to pick top people who don't want to go to a large university. Alfred had a knack for sizing up young men and women, for knowing who would be successful here. That's what he did and he did it very well."

"I assume he's the person who convinced Heinz Gruner to attend Rimson."

"Without checking records I couldn't say for sure, but it's possible."

"How would that work, Dean Hershey?"

"He might have a guidance counselor select a few seniors for him to talk to early in the senior year or even during the junior year. He would see their transcripts, talk to them, decide that this one or that one would be a good Rimson student, and follow up with letters and phone calls. This wasn't a full-time job, you understand; it was something he enjoyed doing. He brought us a number of fine students."

"Did he check on them after they became students?"

I asked, remembering the letter that said that K had come to the campus.

"When he was teaching here, he saw those students frequently. I don't honestly know if he kept up with them after he left for Columbia."

I thanked him for giving me the inside story on Alfred Koch. Then I got ready to go into New York for my appointment with the man himself.

24

I saw to it that I did not arrive before eleven thirty. I was fortunate to find a parking meter on Broadway, which gave me exactly an hour including walking to and from Koch's office. I didn't think he wanted me to take up his lunch hour, so I was confident I would make it back in time.

I climbed the stairs as I had the last time, knocked on the door, heard him call "Enter," and went inside. This time he greeted me a little more warmly, indicating to me that he wanted something that he thought I could give him.

"Enjoying our good weather?" he began.

"Very much. Is the semester over now?"

"Ah yes, semester over, grades turned in, crowds gone. This is when I take the most pleasure in being here."

"What was it you wanted to talk to me about?" I asked so that we would not spend our time together talking about the weather and the empty campus.

"I've been giving a lot of thought to Heinz Gruner and his untimely death, especially since Hilda died. As I think I told you, we were acquaintances from the Old Country."

"I remember."

"And Heinz's accident destroyed his parents, as you can imagine. He was their only child; all their hopes and dreams rested on him."

"Yes."

"Hilda was very concerned that Heinz had committed suicide."

"She told me that. Before she died I was able to determine to my satisfaction that that didn't happen. I told her his death was an accident."

"But you don't believe it was an accident."

"Something was going on, Professor Koch. There were people living on that corridor who went hiking with him, and I believe one or more of them caused the accident."

"Do you have proof of that?"

"I have proof to my satisfaction that at least one other student was on that mountain. I think there may well have been two."

"That's quite a stretch from a young man walking alone, as he told his parents he wanted to do."

"How do you know that?" I asked.

"I spoke to them, of course, after I heard of his death."

"And they said he was walking alone."

"Yes. The trip, as you may know, was a birthday present from them."

"I know."

"So using frail circumstantial evidence to 'prove' that another person or persons were there doesn't count for much."

"It doesn't count for much to you, Professor. When I'm done, I'll have a solid case to turn over to the Arizona sheriff's department." His overbearing attitude was bringing out the worst in me. "It may interest you to know that my husband is a lieutenant in NYPD. We have discussed this in depth." I rarely pull out Jack's job and status, but this man really irritated me.

"I see." He tapped a yellow pencil on his desktop. "So you really don't know firsthand that anyone was on that trail with Heinz."

"I have enough evidence that my police contact in Arizona is interested."

"Mm-hmm."

"I understand you were a scout for Rimson College at one time and you recruited Heinz."

"Who did you hear that from?"

"I'd rather not divulge my sources."

"Yes, I did scout for Rimson. Even now an occasional parent calls and asks me about the college."

"Heinz expected to go to Harvard."

He leaned back. When he wasn't leading the conversation, he was reluctant to provide any information. "He had his eye on Harvard, that's true. Actually, his father wanted him to go there. Heinz preferred a smaller institution."

"Did he apply to Harvard?"

"You know, Miss Bennett, these things are not your business."

"I am making them my business in order to determine who killed my old acquaintance."

"I don't know whether he applied or not."

I was sure he had. Why else would he have said in the blurb under his yearbook picture that he intended to go there? "Do you know who the other people on the mountain were?"

"How could I possibly know that?" He was becoming as irritated with me as I was with him.

"Because I'm sure you knew people at Rimson, and one of them might have known."

"I would like to ask you about a couple of people who were on Heinz's corridor that semester," he said, ignoring my comment.

"Go ahead."

"I believe you mentioned you've been in touch with Professor Fallon."

"I have."

"And he's given you much of your inside information. Have you also talked to Andrew Franklin?"

"I have."

"What did he tell you?"

"That he helped Heinz down the stairs with two pieces of luggage."

"Did you speak to Arthur Howell?"

"Yes." I began to see where this was going. He would ask about some people who were not on the mountain with Heinz and lead in to the important ones.

"And he said?"

"He said he was the last man out of the dorm that year. He was working on a paper."

"Did you verify his statement?"

"To my satisfaction." I hate to lie, but this was one time that I did. I had not been able to think of a way to check on Howell.

"Howell had a roommate named Steven Millman."

Now we were getting to his point. I made a show of looking at my notes. "That's correct."

"When did you speak to him?"

"Last week."

"Did you call him?"

"He called me."

"How did he get your number?"

"I used an intermediary."

"Whose name is?"

"That's my business."

"Miss Bennett , I can't help you if you keep secrets."

"Professor Koch, you invited me here today. I assumed you intended to give me information. How could it possibly matter how I came to speak to Steve Millman?"

"Did Arthur Howell give you his number or make the arrangement for you to speak to Millman?" He was barely controlling his anger now.

"I think that my intermediary is privileged information until I turn over what I have to the police." I looked at my watch. It was after noon. "I assume you're curious because Steve Millman has kept his whereabouts a secret since that summer."

"I don't know what you're talking about. I'm sure the alumni office has his address."

"They don't. Is there anything else?"

"Did you speak to Martin McHugh?"

"I not only spoke to him, I had lunch with him. And I talked to Barry Woodson and to Eric Goode and to some others. What exactly are you trying to find out?"

"Nothing. I think we're done."

I dropped my notebook back in my bag and said good-bye. As I walked back to the car, I felt grateful that I hadn't parked in a garage for ten or fifteen times as much as the meter. All I had gotten from our conversation was that Koch was nervous about my talking to Steve and Marty. To me that meant that those two men knew something about Koch, and Koch didn't want me to find out what that was.

As I drove home it occurred to me that Heinz's old friend from high school, Don Shiller, might know something about whether Heinz had applied to Harvard and why he hadn't gone. I couldn't think how this affected his trip to Arizona and his subsequent death, but the issue seemed to bother Koch, which made it potentially interesting.

I would call Don that night.

"Don," I said when I reached him that evening, "I have some questions that no one else can answer but you might be able to."

"I'll give it a try. Why do you think I have answers?"

"Because you were Heinz's best friend, and best friends confide in each other."

"True. What do you want to know?"

"The yearbook says that Heinz wanted to go to Harvard."

"Yeah, that was a big deal in his life and in his family. His father had his heart set on Harvard. He was a pretty authoritarian man—not to say he wasn't a loving father—but this was what he wanted for his son."

"Did Heinz apply?"

"Definitely."

"Was he turned down?"

"That's one of the questions I can't answer. I know there was a lot of discussion about where he was going when those envelopes were delivered. I think Rimson offered him a scholarship, and that may have been what made the decision."

"You said Heinz's father had his heart set on Harvard. How did Heinz feel about it? Was his heart set on Harvard, too?"

"You know, I don't think so. We talked a lot about where we wanted to go. For a while, he was enthralled with Harvard. They drove up there between our junior and senior years. He thought the campus was great, the city was great. He was interviewed, though, and I'm not sure the interview went all that well. You remember Heinz. He was quiet and shy. It took awhile till he came out of his shell and I don't think the interviewer had the skills to do it. Or maybe he didn't care. Maybe he just made up his mind that this kid wasn't Harvard material.

"They came back from Boston, and Heinz wasn't talking about Harvard so much anymore. He started talking about Rimson. One weekend he and his father flew to Illinois for a visit. When they came back, there was a lot of discord in the family. Heinz was very circumspect, especially where his parents were concerned. I could tell something had happened but I knew better than to ask about it."

"Did he tell you what he thought of Rimson?"

"He loved the campus. They offered the kinds of courses he was interested in. And I think they gave him a scholarship."

"How did he become interested?" I persisted.

"Some guy, some relative or something, came to the high school and singled him out."

"I know I asked you this before, but could that man's name have been Alfred Koch?"

"I wouldn't know. I don't think Heinz ever mentioned it. Anyway, he was glad he made the choice, even if his father wasn't."

"Mrs. Gruner showed me old letters from Heinz to his parents shortly before she died. In one of them Heinz refers to a man he calls K. When I asked her who this was, she become unhinged. She took the letter and more or less threw me out. At that time I had no idea who he was, but her reaction was so strong, so negative—"

"It may have reminded her of an unhappy time in their lives."

"I'm told she left whatever money she had to Rimson. She must have decided at some point that Heinz had made a good decision and was happy there."

"She wasn't as involved in that college decision as her husband was. He just had this dream that his son would go to Harvard. I'll tell you something else. I have a feeling money was involved."

"You mean the cost of tuition?" I asked.

"No, I mean to get Heinz into Harvard."

"I see," I said, although I didn't see clearly. "That could account for her anger."

"And maybe her shame," Don said. "That they had to pay to get Heinz into college."

"Don, you've been very helpful. I'll let you know how this turns out."

"I'll keep thinking about it. Something else may come back."

I said that I hoped it would.

25

Koch had taken money from the Gruners, possibly a bribe, possibly a fee, depending on their arrangement. It sounded more like a bribe to me. If he was a scout for Rimson, what was he doing trying to get someone into Harvard?

I could believe that Heinz would not interview well. And although he did well in high school, it was possible that his SATs weren't good enough. Smart people are sometimes poor test takers. And the Gruners might not have sent him to special classes to increase his scores, thinking that he was bright and would fare well without assistance. But what did all of this have to do with Heinz's death? And who might know what filled the gaps in Don's story?

By ten Tuesday morning I decided I wasn't going to hear from Marty McHugh on my request for a private conversation with Steve Millman. That meant I could not confirm that I had spoken to Millman himself. It also meant, I thought, that Marty was involved in the hike on the mountain. But whether Heinz had wanted Harvard over Rimson, whether Marty had been accused of plagiarism in his second year or fourth year, I still couldn't see a motive for either of those people to want to harm Heinz.

I did mindless things around the house, then in the garden, which I preferred, trying to think of someone I hadn't talked to who might still shed light on this case. And then a name popped into my head. I had spoken only briefly to Dr. Farley, the executor of Mrs. Gruner's will. If she appointed him to fulfill that important task, she must have had great faith in him and perhaps some affection to go along with it. I called Hillside Village and made an appointment to see him at eleven.

I then called Dean Hershey and asked a question that had been bothering me since my conversation with Don Shiller the night before. "I have heard on good authority that Professor Koch promised to get Heinz Gruner into Harvard."

"I think your authority is not reliable."

Ignoring his comment, I continued, "I have also heard that Professor Koch took money from Heinz's parents to accomplish that."

"If that's true, it was a betrayal of the college's trust and most certainly unethical. Heinz didn't get into Harvard, as I heard the story. And what you're saying sounds like a bribe, and that could possibly be illegal. Especially if he failed."

"That's what I'm thinking."

"May I ask who told you this?"

"Heinz's oldest friend from high school."

"I see."

"Was Professor Koch paid to scout for Rimson?"

"It was part of his duties. He taught fewer classes than normal and had a schedule that accommodated travel. We paid his expenses, of course. But if you mean did he receive a bounty for bringing in students, the answer is definitely not."

"Do you know if Professor Koch had contacts at Harvard?"

"I'm sure he had contacts at many top universities. He was well known in his field, he attended conferences, he had gone to school with people who ended up on faculties around the country. I'm sure he knew people at Harvard."

"Thank you, Dean Hershey."

"Miss Bennett, what on earth does this have to do with Heinz's death?"

"I wish I knew. It's just something that I became aware of in my investigation."

We left it at that. A little later, I drove over to Hillside Village and waited in the lobby till Dr. Farley came down the corridor to see me.

"How are you doing, Mrs. Brooks?"

"Pretty good," I said as we began to walk toward his office. "I've made progress in my search for answers in the death of Mrs. Gruner's son, and it occurred to me you might be able to fill in some gaps."

"It's possible." He unlocked the door to his office, pushed it open, and let me walk inside first. Then we took seats in the two guest chairs. "How can I help you?"

I gave him a little background, reminding him of his job of mediator shortly before Mrs. Gruner died.

"I remember that. We didn't discuss the substance of her anger but we made a kind of peace."

"For which I was very grateful. Now I'd like to talk to you about the substance. I think Mrs. Gruner may at some point in your relationship have told you things that could help me get to the bottom of this case."

"It's possible," he said once again.

"I'm sure she told you the circumstances of her son's death."

"She did. It marked the beginning of the decline of her family. Her husband died a year or so later, and she had a stroke after that that left her incapacitated. She made good physical progress in her recovery, thanks to her strong will, but her spirit was crushed from the moment she heard about the boy's death."

"I can understand that. Let's go back a bit in time to

when her son was applying to colleges. Did she talk to you about that?"

Dr. Farley looked across the room, then nodded. "She did. I have to think about this. Give me a minute."

He didn't go to a file drawer to find a document so I assumed his conversation with her had been informal. "There was something that troubled her, some difficulty her son had. He wanted to go to one school but wasn't accepted. He chose another."

"He wanted to go to Harvard," I said. "His father wanted him to go to Harvard."

"Yes, that's it. It was the father. I never met Mr. Gruner, of course. He died before Hilda had her stroke. But yes, he wanted the son to go to Harvard and they made some connection, a friend or relative, who said he could make it happen. Wait a minute. It was more than that. He asked for a fee to accomplish the acceptance."

"Do you recall how much he charged?"

"It's too long ago, but it was a lot of money, at least to the Gruners, thousands of dollars."

"That would be a lot of money for me, too," I said.

"And when it didn't work out, he refused to return it. Maybe he gave them a few hundred back but he said he had incurred large expenses in his futile attempt. She never forgave him. To hear her tell the story, it could have happened yesterday. She felt betrayed. Her husband was beyond consolation. Interestingly, the son seemed happy to go to Rimson, the other school."

"Did they threaten to sue this man?" I asked.

"Dignity was very important to the family. To sue

237

would be to admit that they had bribed someone to get their son into Harvard and they couldn't do that. They wouldn't do that."

"She left her money to Rimson College," I said.

"Yes. We talked about that. She felt the son had gotten a fine education there, that he was happy there and that the library should benefit. As you know, I'm in the process of adjusting the endowment set up in his memory."

"Do you remember anything else about the man who took the money?"

"He taught at Rimson. The family had known him from Germany. I'm not sure I recall anything else."

"Why did Mrs. Gruner tell you about this, Dr. Farley?"

"She wasn't a very outgoing person. I think she was looking for a confidant, someone who would listen, someone she could trust, a person who would not be judgmental. I would not have told you these things if she were still alive."

"I understand."

"It was something that she never stopped thinking about."

I knew that was true. She had said as much to me. I thanked him for telling me. He went on to assure me that he was taking no fee himself for his work on her will. Every cent would go to the Rimson Library. I decided I had finally found an honest man.

I was eating a late lunch when the phone rang. I

reached over and picked it up, moving my salad out of the way.

A man's voice said, "Is this Christine Bennett Brooks?"

"Yes, it is."

"This is Steven Millman."

"Yes. Hello."

"Marty McHugh doesn't know I'm calling. I'm using a throwaway device and you won't be able to trace the call. If you tell McHugh we have spoken, I can assure you I will know and we will never speak again."

"I have no intention of telling him."

"I know some details about Heinz Gruner's death that no one else will tell you. I haven't decided how much— if anything—I'm going to tell you. But you have to convince me that what you know stays with you."

"You're putting me in a difficult position, Mr. Millman," I said. "I don't intend to tell Marty McHugh, but if I learn that Heinz was murdered, I'm bound by my conscience and the law to tell the police."

"Heinz wasn't murdered."

"Can you prove that to me?"

"Probably not, but I can tell you what I know. You can believe it or not as you choose."

Something struck me as he spoke. "Does Marty know what you know?"

"Some of it. I'm probably the only person alive who knows the whole story. But other people know parts of it."

"Mr. Millman, you know I'm interested. I knew Heinz

239

in high school. I met his mother recently, in the last month of her life. The pain of the loss of her son never diminished. I believe I convinced her that he didn't commit suicide, which was her greatest fear. But if someone was responsible for his death—"

"Someone was."

"I want to know."

"How will you benefit from finding out?"

For a moment, I didn't quite understand his question. "Do you mean will I make money from learning the truth? I won't. I wouldn't try to. All I know is that something terrible happened that day on Picacho Peak and if I can find out what it was, perhaps I can make some good come out of that day."

"I will tell you one thing today, something you've already guessed. I was on the mountain when Heinz fell."

"Thank you."

"I can't say anything—" The line was suddenly silent and I realized his phone or card had run out of time. He had given me one small fact that I already knew, and now I would have to wait to see whether he would ever call again.

I hung up and sat there, wondering if Steve had another phone card, but after a few minutes I pulled my salad over and began to eat again. Steve Millman had made contact and that was surprising and rewarding. Now I had to wait.

Mel called when she got home from school. Both her

kids were at activities in town, and she wanted to sit and chat and enjoy the fine weather. I told her to come over and I put the kettle on the stove. Eddie was also doing something at a friend's house, which gave us an hour or so to relax without children present.

We sat at the patio table under the umbrella, feeling a pleasant breeze, and I listened to a tale of Mel's mother, whom I knew, and she listened to an update of my case.

"How did he find you?" Mel asked when I had told her of my call earlier in the day.

"I think I gave him my full name and he knows approximately where I live, so between the Internet and trial and error, he got my number."

"And he admits to being on the mountain that day."

"It's not much of an admission, Mel. He's been my main suspect since I found out he lived in Phoenix and dropped out of Rimson after that semester."

"But he told you a different story last time you spoke. Now he's coming clean."

"That's what it looks like. I hope there's going to be another call and he'll come cleaner."

"Why won't he say these things to you in front of that other fellow, the one who took you to lunch?"

"I don't know. I assume Steve is going to implicate him in some way."

"So this other guy—"

"McHugh."

"Killed your friend and won't let Steve disclose what he knows."

"Steve said there was no murder."

241

"Sounds like there's more to the story, Chris."

"This is one story that doesn't seem to have an end." I poured more tea. "I think it's getting to be time for iced tea."

"Right. And homemade lemonade. I always use ice cubes made of the tea so it doesn't dilute."

"Good idea. Jack will appreciate having something tasty in the fridge in hot weather." I leaned toward the house, thinking I had heard a sound.

"What's up?"

"Thought that was my phone. I don't want to miss Steve if he calls back. If I don't answer, he may give up."

"He's not going to give up, Chris," Mel said. "He's made a big decision. It's taken him twenty years to come to this point. He wants to get something off his chest and you're going to be the one who hears it."

"I'm glad he said there was no murder. I didn't exactly promise not to tell anyone, but I have to go to the police if there's a cause and I don't want to betray a trust."

"You'll work it out. It won't be the first time."

If there hadn't been a murder, it had to have been an accident. If it was an accident, I didn't have to give my information to the police. I decided that some argument must have taken place among the three young men on the mountain. Steve was not the most likable fellow from what I had heard, and Marty had lied to me about the plagiarism to make his story more poignant. It had certainly worked on me, but discovering the lie had turned me completely against him. He had a beef with Steve Millman, and Steve Millman was angry with him. Heinz wanted to hike in the mountains and ended up with two companions who disliked each other. It must have been an unpleasant day to say the least. Which of the two had taken the suitcases? Which had taken the little backpack and returned it in time for the Towers to find it? There were still many unanswered questions.

26

"He called you?" Jack was astounded. "That's not usual for a killer."

"He said there was no murder."

"When did a killer say anything else?"

"If he'd killed Heinz, I hardly think he would call me and talk about it. Something's going on there and he wants to clear his name."

"By using you."

"In a way, yes."

"So that leaves McHugh. Unless there was a real crowd on that mountain."

I smiled. "Three's enough of a crowd. Can you drink iced coffee tonight?"

"Sounds good."

"Mel mentioned how to make iced tea, so I brewed a bunch of coffee and froze coffee ice cubes."

"Sounds like a treat."

We drank it out of tall crystal glasses that I had inherited from my aunt. I still had some in my glass when the phone rang. It was right beside me so I pressed the button and said hello.

"This is Steve."

"Yes, Steve." I saw Jack perk up.

"Do you know who was on the mountain that day?"

"You, Heinz, and Marty McHugh."

"You knew Marty McHugh was there."

"I figured it out."

"You're short one man."

"There was a fourth man on the hike?"

"Yes. There was one more."

I had a sudden terrible feeling that the fourth man was Herb Fallon. "Who was he?" I asked.

"It's one of the people you've been talking to. I'm sure he won't admit it. But there were four of us who went up and three of us who came down."

"Tell me what happened to Heinz's suitcases," I said, since he didn't seem to want to disclose the fourth name.

"They were in my car because he had stayed at my house, and he wasn't coming back."

"Where was he going?"

"I think he wanted to go down to Tombstone."

"How did he plan to get there?"

"He had a ride."

"With Marty or the other man?"

"With one of them."

"So there were two cars."

"My car and someone else's."

"I'd like to know who the fourth man was," I said.

"I'm not ready to tell you. I'm not sure I'll ever be ready."

"But Marty McHugh knows."

"He'll never even admit that he was there. And I told you: you say anything to him and that's the end of our conversations."

"I won't say anything," I promised again. "But I want to know who the fourth man was."

The line went dead. I was left with a phone in my hand and an unanswered question hanging in the air.

"You're up to four guys?" Jack asked after I turned the phone off.

"That's what he says."

"You think he's making this up? It's getting to sound like a party, not a hike in the mountains."

I told him what Steve had said. "I'm afraid it's Herb Fallon. Some of the things he told me don't agree with what I learned myself. The more I learned on my own, the less often he called. He may be worried that I'm putting together a scenario that includes him. Of course he'll deny being there. And if these three men keep quiet, there's no one else alive who can tell me the truth."

"But Millman may talk."

"But why, Jack? If he was partly responsible for Heinz's death, what would motivate him to talk when the others won't?"

"Think about what you just said and maybe you'll

come up with an answer."

I picked up the coffee glasses and took them to the kitchen, where I washed and dried them and put them away. People talked about the blue wall of silence put up by the police department. I felt as though I had just run into a similar wall made of Rimson students. They were all protecting themselves, and in doing so they were protecting one another. Why would Steve Millman break the bond?

I found myself thinking about it as I tried to fall asleep later that night. The three men were on the mountain when Heinz fell. They were horrified when it happened but the slope was too steep to negotiate, as it had been for Joseph and me. Heinz did not move, and the men feared he was dead or dying. Worse, they knew that if he survived, he would tell a tale that would implicate them in his accident. So they ran, leaving him to die. One of them picked up his backpack and took it along with no thought to whether he would keep it, throw it away, or return it to the site.

In the parking lot they made a pact that none of them would ever tell the story of the accident. Steve Millman drove home in his mother's car. Herb and Marty, who had probably rented a car intending to drive to Tombstone with Heinz, returned the car and flew home. Steve's mother had not expected the guests to return so she asked no questions. Probably Heinz's suitcases were in the Millman car.

It sounded like a good story. I just couldn't figure out why Steve was now speaking out. And I knew I could no longer call Herb Fallon because he would tell Steve or Marty that I knew there were four of them, and Steve might suffer repercussions.

I was so close, but I wasn't there yet. And my lines of communication were now blocked. I was at the mercy of Steve Millman, who might never call back.

The next morning, after my men left, I was trying to make sense of what I knew and what I wished I knew when the phone rang. Steve, I thought, hurrying to pick it up.

"Chris, this is Herb Fallon."

I felt a moment of panic. "Herb, hi. What's up?"

"Just wanted to tell you. My wife and I are on our way to New York in a couple of hours for a few days of good food, theater, and music. I could meet you for cocktails tomorrow evening if you're available. My wife'll be shopping or recovering from shopping, so it'll just be you and me. We can talk."

I knew there was nothing on our calendar, but I felt uncomfortable meeting him alone. "Sure," I said. "Where were you planning to be?"

"I always like the lobby of the Waldorf-Astoria. I'll get us a table and keep an eye out for you. How's five?"

"Five is fine."

"You have a cell?"

"No. But I'll be there."

"Great. Just look for a bully."

I called Jack when I hung up.

"I'll meet you there," he said. "At the Lexington

Avenue entrance. He'll be on the Park Avenue side. You can go on ahead and I'll keep watch. It's a public place and he's not going to do anything, but I'll feel better if I'm there."

So would I. "Great. I'll call Elsie."

"Why don't we make an evening of it? We haven't been out to dinner for a while."

"That sounds terrific."

His suggestion made me feel much better. Whatever happened during our meeting, I had dinner with Jack to look forward to. And despite the fact that Herb and I would meet in a very public place, knowing that Jack was nearby made me feel safer. I just had my fingers crossed that no emergency arose in Midtown South that would keep him from getting to the Waldorf by five.

I guessed that this meeting was Herb's way of finding out what I knew and whether I had him on my suspect list. I would have to be careful what I said to keep him thinking he was my number one informant, and not suspect number three.

While I was having lunch, Steve Millman called.

"Sorry for these abrupt conversations," he said, "but I'm using a phone card and it runs out without warning. You were asking me who the fourth man was when last night's card expired."

"Yes. I'd like to know."

"It's someone you've talked to."

"Did I tell you that?" The truth was, I couldn't remember what I'd told him.

"I don't remember. Marty briefed me at some length

before we spoke the first time. His name is in my notes."

"Will you give it to me?"

"I'm still concerned about retribution."

"Steve, let's be honest," I said. "You're calling me. You have something you want to get off your chest."

"That's true."

"You said there was no murder."

"That's true, too. But there might have been."

"There might have been a murder if what?"

"If things had gone as planned."

"There was a plan and it wasn't carried out?"

"That's it."

I kept waiting each time he stopped talking to see if he would elaborate with something more than these brief comments, but he wasn't biting. "Tell me about the plagiarism."

"I don't want to talk about it."

"I talked to Professor Addison."

"How'd you find him?"

"I've done a lot of work, Steve. His name came up."

"What did he say?"

"That one of you plagiarized the other."

"He really said that?"

"Steve, I need to know who the fourth man on the mountain was."

"I'm still thinking about that. There was someone who—let's just say there was someone I had a justifiable complaint against."

"And he was on the mountain with you?"

"Yeah. Look, I've gotta go. I'll think about what else I want to tell you."

I was getting tired of this. If he was making these calls to have some fun at my expense, I would be very annoyed, but how would I know?

When Eddie came home, the weather had turned hot and humid, and I decided we could give the town pool a try. The water might still be cool, but I was aching to do some laps. We changed our clothes and drove over, finding a couple of lounges in a shady place. And then we were off. Eddie was like a fish. He would take his deep-end swimming test as soon as I felt he was ready, and from the way he was moving through the water, I thought that would be very soon. Over the weekend, I would get Jack's opinion.

Finally Eddie left the pool and joined a game with other small children while I got my wish and swam several laps, enjoying stretching those muscles for the first time of the year.

In the evening, Jack and I discussed our plans for the next afternoon. I would take the train to Manhattan so that we would have only one car to drive home. The Waldorf-Astoria covered a full block between Forty-ninth and Fiftieth and between Park Avenue and Lex. The cocktail area was on the Park Avenue side so we would meet at the Lexington entrance and ride the escalator up to the lobby floor; while I walked through the entire lobby, Jack would hang back, eventually standing where he had a view of our table.

"If he wants to walk you out, I'll be right behind

you," he said. "I just showed up to meet you for dinner."

"OK."

"I doubt whether he's staying there. It's a bit pricey for a college professor."

"I can always tell him I'm meeting my husband and he'll be on his way."

"So we'll meet at five to five on Lex."

"I'll be there."

27

Grand Central Station sits on top of what would be Park Avenue except that the divided avenue splits to pass alongside the east and west sides of the building. The avenue to the east of Park is Lexington and I got myself over there, walked up to the Waldorf, and waited at the north end of the entrance. In this new casual society of ours, I saw more people dressed in sporty attire than in cocktail clothes or business wear. I guess if you're spending your vacation shopping, you may as well be comfortable.

I was early, but not by much. I scanned Lex in both directions but didn't see Jack. It got to be five of and then a minute before five. I became nervous. It was one of the times I would have liked to have a cell phone with me. Jack carries one because he has to be available virtually twenty-four hours a day. But I don't, and I tremble to think what our monthly bill would be.

Five o'clock and no sign of my husband. It was too

late to call the precinct; besides, he was surely on his way by now, probably backed up in rush-hour traffic or having trouble finding a garage. At three minutes past, I stepped into the middle of the sidewalk and looked in both directions. Jack wasn't visible, and I had no choice but to keep my appointment. I went inside, rode up the long escalator, and started through the lobby—past shops where I could afford nothing, elevators to the many floors, finally arriving at the Park Avenue end where a huge chandelier hung over a mosaic of the wheel of life. I glanced back but saw no familiar face.

To my right were a couple of levels of tables and chairs with waiters dancing from one to another. I scanned the faces of the men, trying to find one big man sitting alone looking for me. Finally a short, round man with glasses and dark hair, wearing a brown suit, stood and looked directly at me. Could that possibly be my bully?

I took a last look behind me for Jack, who wasn't there. Herb waved and I smiled and walked toward his table. He made his way in my direction and we met about halfway.

"Chris?" He was five-four or -five, slightly shorter than I.

"Herb," I said, almost relieved at his size. "Nice to meet you."

"I've got a table. Let's sit."

Unfortunately, the chair he led me to faced Park Avenue, so I would have no way of seeing Jack without being obvious. I sat and gave my order of white wine to the waiter, who had materialized in seconds.

"Well it's great to meet you," Herb said, "after all our phone calls. You find this place all right?"

I assured him I had.

"So what've you learned since we last discussed Heinz's death?"

"I can't even remember what I've told you," I said. "I learn a little more every day, but I don't have it down yet. There were at least three men on the mountain. Did I tell you that?"

"I'm not sure. Who was the third?"

"It has to be Marty McHugh."

"Marty flew to Arizona?"

"It looks that way. I told you I had a conference call with Steve Millman."

"Yeah. With Marty on the line."

"Marty wanted to make sure Steve didn't drop anything that would hurt him."

"Right. So you think they killed Heinz."

"I don't know what to think. And it's possible there was a fourth person there."

"Another one! Hey, you'll have the whole college on that trail pretty soon."

My wine came and I took a sip. It was cool and crisp. Herb was drinking Scotch on the rocks with a twist, something that would have appealed to Jack.

"Not quite," I said in response to his comment.

"What makes you think there were more than three?"

"Something I came across yesterday," I said lamely.

"Everyone's been lying to me, Herb. Well, not Dean Hershey."

"And not me."

"No, of course not. You've given me lots of good information. But Marty lied about some things. Steve told me things that were clearly not true. Andrew Franklin I'm not sure of. It depends on something that Steve said."

"But those may be details. What we need to know is who was on that mountain and who had it in for Heinz."

"Yes. I've also spoken to Heinz's oldest friend from high school. He read me some of Heinz's letters that were written that last semester. Your name is mentioned."

"What did he say about me?" Was it eagerness or concern that I heard in his voice?

"Not a lot."

"He didn't say I was taking that trip, did he?"

I felt a chill. "No, he didn't. He may have said that he asked you but you couldn't make it."

"That sounds about right."

So I had worked my way out of that. I wanted desperately to look over my shoulder and see if my husband's reassuring presence was there, but I didn't dare. I sipped my wine and waited for Herb to pick up the dialogue.

"Well, I can say you've learned a lot in the last few days. How long are you giving this?"

"I'm not sure. I may need to get back to Professor Addison again. I really appreciate that lead."

"No trouble."

I looked at my watch. It was almost twenty-five after and I was out of things to tell him.

"Why don't we hop a cab and go to my hotel? I'd like you to meet my wife. I'm sure she's there by now."

"I would love to, but I really can't. My husband's meeting me here soon. He said as long as I was in the city, why didn't we go out to dinner? So that's what we're doing."

"I wish we could join you, but we have tickets over on the west side. And I need a shower and a change of clothes before I go anywhere."

"Maybe another time." I sipped more wine. He had finished his drink, so I assumed our meeting was coming to an end.

"Where's your husband meeting you?"

"Under that huge chandelier. I guess half of New York must meet there."

"It's really something."

I chanced a glance at that area, knowing Jack would not be standing in the middle of the lobby.

"He there yet?"

I shook my head. "Any minute."

"Well, I guess I'd better get going. It's been great meeting you, Chris." He pulled out a wallet and put some bills on the table. The check had mysteriously appeared.

"Same here." I stood, and we started for the center of the lobby. "Thank you so much for the drink. I'm so glad to be able to put a person to the voice."

We shook hands and I watched him go down the stairs to the Park Avenue entrance. He turned and waved. I waved back, then pivoted.

"I'm right here," Jack said. He leaned over and kissed me. I felt like hugging him. "Sorry I was late. As usual, something came up and I was thirty seconds too late getting out of there. The desk officer grabbed me and I didn't get here till five fifteen."

"I'm just so relieved to see you, I've forgotten all about it."

"Let's go back to Lex. I've got a reservation a couple of blocks from here."

I grabbed his arm and hung on to it as we walked back the way I had come.

"I don't know if he's the one, Jack," I said when we were sitting at a table with a heavy white linen table-cloth and huge napkins. "I was so nervous, I hardly knew what I was saying. But I didn't disclose that I've been talking to Steve Millman. Did you see the size of him?"

"Short and squat. That's your bully."

"I was looking for tall and powerful. What a surprise. He invited me to his hotel to meet his wife. I'm glad I had a legitimate excuse for not going."

"Do you seriously think he was part of the group that killed your friend?"

"I seriously think it's possible."

"It looks like your only hope is to get this Steve Millman guy to tell you what he knows."

"He hasn't called for two days."

"Two days isn't forever," my husband assured me. "Let's look at the menu. This place was recommended highly by my captain."

"Good. Now that I'm here, I'm starving."

The idea came to me while we were driving home. I kept it to myself. Having botched the meeting with Herb Fallon, I didn't want to say anything to Jack until I had something firm. Tomorrow morning I had an important call to make.

At ten on Friday morning I called Dean Hershey. I started out by saying that I had met Herb Fallon in New York, and how nice it was to know what he looked like and discuss the case with him in person.

"What I would like to know this morning," I said when we had finished our introductory chitchat, "is the names of the other students in Heinz's class who were brought to Rimson by Professor Koch."

"Ah, I wonder if that's in our files."

"It's become quite important," I said.

"I could probably call him and ask. He might remember. It was his last year at Rimson."

"I'd rather you didn't ask him personally, Dean Hershey. Or even let him know that you're looking into it."

"Let me see what I can find."

I called Joseph after that and told her what I had learned in the last few days and what I had asked the dean to find out for me.

"That sounds like a good question, Chris. Let me know when you get the answer."

I shopped, made lunch, sat down to eat . . . and the phone rang.

"This is Dean Hershey. I've found the answer to your question."

"Thank you. I'm listening." I picked up a pencil and grabbed an envelope with a bill in it.

"There were two other students that year, Erica Wright and Steven Millman."

"Steve," I said.

"I think we established that he dropped out of Rimson after Heinz's death. And we haven't heard from him since."

"I have, but he hasn't been as forthcoming as I'd like. He was on the trail with Heinz the day of the accident."

"I see. What does that have to do with Alfred?"

"I'm not sure. Do you have a phone number for Erica Wright?"

He dictated it. Her married name was Tyler, she lived in Buffalo, and, he told me, had graduated with honors from Rimson. "Alfred knew how to pick them."

"Thank you very much," I said sincerely. "This is a big help."

I pushed aside my salad and dialed the Buffalo number. A woman answered immediately and said she was Erica Tyler. I gave her some background, and she told me she remembered that Heinz had died.

"I understand you came to Rimson partly through the

work of a professor who scouted for appropriate students," I said.

"Professor Koch, yes. He came to my high school and I made a good impression on him. Rimson was always my first choice, so I was really pleased that he wanted me to go there."

"Did your parents pay him for his help?"

"I don't think so. I think he just met me and picked me as a prospect."

"Did you know Steve Millman and Heinz Gruner?"

"I knew Heinz slightly. I knew Steve better, although he was a pain in the neck, an annoying person. He complained about everything. He really disliked Professor Koch, although I think the professor wasn't even at Rimson the year we were freshmen."

"He went to Columbia," I volunteered.

"But he popped up one day during the year to see how we were all doing."

"Do you know why Steve disliked him so much?"

"It's so long ago, it probably doesn't matter if I tell you. I think Professor Koch charged Steve's parents a lot of money to get him into Rimson. It was Steve's first or second choice and I don't think he had the grades, although his SATs were good. There was something going on there. You know what? I think Steve or his family were planning to take Professor Koch to court. Steve used the word 'bribe' when he talked about it. He also said Koch had taken bribes from a number of students' families."

"I see. Do you know if it ever went to court?"

"I don't think it did. Heinz died and Steve dropped out, and I never heard anything more about it."

I gave her my phone number in case she remembered anything else and went back to my lunch. That and what Dean Hershey had told me were my missing pieces of information. It just didn't explain why Heinz Gruner had fallen off the trail. And if Steve Millman didn't call back, I might never know.

28

Erica Tyler called me back late in the afternoon.

"You got me thinking," she said. "I called my mother and asked her if they paid Professor Koch to get me into Rimson. The answer is yes."

"Really," I said.

"My parents were annoyed. They felt that I could get in on my own but he made a case that it was still harder for girls, that the number of applicants had grown in the last few years. Anyway, he said he had expenses and asked them for a thousand dollars, and they gave him half with the promise of the second half when I was accepted."

"Did they pay it?"

"She said they actually talked about not paying it but felt they had made a commitment, so yes, they gave it to him."

"This is very interesting and helpful. Just to set the record straight, it was unethical of him to demand money for what Rimson paid him to do."

"I'm not surprised, but getting into college was such an anxious affair, I can understand why they caved in."

I was tempted to call Koch and tell him what I knew, but I sensed that was not the way to go. If there was a criminal case, Jack would know how to handle it better than I with his police and law background. In the meantime, I would hope that Steve would call and fill in the narrowing gaps in my information. It had been three days since I'd last heard from him, and if he didn't come through, I wasn't sure how I would move forward.

Eddie came home with his friend Terry, and I set them up outside with games and milk and cookies. The phone rang several times, but it was always about something local. I kept my eye on the boys and kept the phone near me. Finally it rang and I heard Steve Millman's voice.

"I've been doing a lot of thinking," he said.

"I'm listening."

"There were four of us on the trail. Heinz had been the first to make plans for the trek. I said I'd join him. We talked about it and Marty McHugh said he'd like to come along. Then the fourth man showed up. I have to tell you—you probably know this already; you've talked to a lot of the guys—I didn't win any awards in college for charm. There were a lot of people I didn't get along with. And there was the plagiarism issue. Marty hated me. Heinz didn't care one way or the other. And then there was this other thing. Anyway, the plan, as I learned as we hiked up the trail, was to give me my comeuppance, knock me down, hurt me, put me in my place. I don't think they meant to kill me, but I could be wrong."

"You were the intended victim?"

"I was it. We got to that place where it happened. We could see down and no one was coming. It curved going up and we couldn't see around the bend. The other guy nodded at Marty and the two of them came at me. Heinz said what's going on? and Marty said keep out of the way. But he didn't. He was like a bulldog, just went at them to keep them from hurting me. That's when it happened. He lost his footing or one of the others accidentally pushed him instead of me and he just flew over the side, rolled down the slope, hit a stand of trees, and stopped. He never moved. I was—I was almost in tears. This guy had saved my life and paid for it with his own.

"We stood there for a while and the third guy said, 'Here's what happened, Millman. McHugh and I saw you get into an argument with Heinz and push him to his death. We are not reporting this to anyone. You will keep quiet about this for the rest of your life or we will testify that we saw you push him. My word will go a lot further than yours with the reputation you have. Is this understood?' Of course I said yes."

"I see," I said. My heart was pounding. Having been at the site, I could envision what had happened. "Who picked up the backpack?"

"I don't remember. You know, it couldn't have been

262

Marty because he flew home that day. I sure as hell didn't."

"Steve," I said, "who was the fourth man?"

"It was that bastard Koch. He had squeezed money out of my parents to get me into Rimson and I wasn't the only one. There were lots of others, but they didn't want to admit it, or their parents didn't. My parents had talked to a lawyer about bringing charges against him; he'd been served with papers. He showed up at my parents' house the day before the hike, trying to sweet-talk them into withdrawing the suit, which they didn't want to do. Koch was afraid that if it got out that he'd taken bribes, there could be lots more lawsuits and his career could be damaged. It was just a coincidence that he turned up the day we all arrived from Rimson. He didn't know McHugh until he got to our house but he must have sensed the animosity between us.

"In the evening, he went out for a walk with McHugh, and when they came back Koch said he would join us at Picacho Peak the next day. It was pretty crude, but he must've thought if he shook me up, we'd forget about the lawsuit. Maybe we would have, but Marty was there, crying about the plagiarism thing, working himself into a rage. They came at me like a couple of bulls."

"It must have been terrible," I agreed. "Did you take Heinz's suitcases with you?"

"They were in my car."

"And you mailed one of them back to the Gruners."

"Right. I disposed of the other one. There was

263

nothing in it that they needed, and I didn't want to pay to send it to New York."

"And that was it," I said, "four men."

"Four men. And that's it. It's over."

"Not so fast," I said. "I have some questions. What happened with the lawsuit?"

"Oh, that. Koch settled out of court and that was the end of it."

"Well, that's good news," I said. "Now I have a question about your identity. You're impossible to find, but you've kept in touch with Marty McHugh. It seems contradictory."

"OK, here's what happened. After the incident on the mountain, I was scared—to death. I thought McHugh might come after me; I thought all kinds of things, some of them irrational. I changed my name legally and tried to lose myself. Then some time passed and I reassessed my situation. I decided I was better off staying in touch with McHugh—keeping tabs on him, so to speak. I knew what had happened on the mountain. I knew who was at fault. Also, I had proof of Koch's shaking down my parents to get me into Rimson, something he wouldn't want made public. So I wasn't in as weak a position as I had originally thought. But I didn't want to make it easy for people like Heinz's parents or the police or someone like you to find me."

"Have you been in touch with Koch?" I asked.

"Never."

"But you talk to Marty."

264

"Occasionally. When I talked to you with him on the line, that was the first time in a couple of years. I agreed to do it to make you go away. He and I agreed that that was in both our interests. Anyway, it's finally over."

"Steve, don't you want to see justice done?"

"What kind of justice? It wasn't murder; it was an accident. No one will prosecute those guys for an accident. As for bribes, I can't imagine anyone gives a damn after more than twenty years. Who will you get to testify?"

"But you're free now, Steve. If we make this public, McHugh and Koch can't touch you. They'll be shamed. It's a small compensation for the death of an innocent person, but it's something that will make their lives unpleasant. Maybe you can embarrass Koch into returning the money he extorted from all those parents."

There was silence and I thought his card had run out again, but then he said, "I'll think about it."

"Please do."

The next silence was the last one. I hung up and turned my attention to the little boys.

I waited until evening to discuss the situation with Jack. He wrote a page of notes and asked a number of questions. One of them was the name and number of Deputy Gonzales. He decided to call him in the morning. Even if there was no prosecutable case, he wanted Gonzales to have all the missing information.

Jack also promised to visit Alfred Koch with me and

talk to him about the bribes he had apparently taken. Jack agreed that there was little chance of taking the case to court at this late date, but he wanted to pressure Koch into returning the bribes he had taken. I was sure Dean Hershey would be able to dig up years of data—the sum might be substantial. I thought that what Koch had taken from the Gruners should be donated to the library fund in memory of Heinz.

The next day was Saturday, and Deputy Gonzales was off for the weekend. The sheriff's department gave Jack his home phone number, and they had a long conversation in the early afternoon.

"Sounds like a good guy," Jack said when he got off the phone. "I told him Millman had moved but he thinks he'll be able to pressure Millman's mother into giving up the new address. People tend to fold when you get them into an interview room with a couple of cops."

"I think Steve lied in our last conversation," I said. "It's a small thing, but the guy isn't very trustworthy. I'm sure he's the one who grabbed the backpack and returned it a couple of days later."

"What makes you think so?"

"Marty McHugh must have left immediately. I can't believe Koch would have stuck around for even one extra day and then made that trek to drop off the backpack. They must have looked through it on the trail and then Steve took it home, thought better of it, and went back by himself to drop it off."

"Makes sense. This guy Koch in on Monday?"

"Yes. He said I could see him at eleven this past Monday but I went at eleven thirty just to inconvenience him. I hate being ordered around by anyone except my son."

Jack laughed but I had a feeling he agreed with me. Jack then called a detective in his command and asked him to research Alfred Koch's movements on the days around Cinco de Mayo the year of Heinz's death. Credit card receipts placing Koch anywhere near Picacho Peak would do fine.

I drove into the city on Monday, parked my car expensively, and met Jack on campus. He was in full uniform, which I thought might make a desirable impression. We arrived at Koch's office a bit after eleven and opened the door after his "Enter" call.

His eyes bulged as he saw Jack. "What is this?" he said, starting to rise out of his chair.

"Professor Koch, I'm Lt. John Brooks. I have some questions to ask you on behalf of the Pinal County sheriff's office in Arizona."

"What?"

"We have evidence that you were present on Picacho Peak when Heinz Gruner fell to his death."

"Nonsense."

"We have evidence that you took bribes from students' families to get them into Rimson College. That includes the Gruners."

"The Gruners are dead. They can't possibly be used against me."

"We have a very credible witness, Professor,

someone who knows the whole story." He was referring to Dr. Farley. Whether his testimony would even be accepted was iffy, but Jack was trying to scare Koch, and it looked as though he was succeeding.

Koch stared at him.

"We have evidence that you were instrumental in causing Mr. Gruner's fall."

"This is all hearsay. This is nonsense. I was nowhere near that place you just mentioned. I wasn't even at Rimson College that year."

"Credit card receipts put you in Phoenix the day of Gruner's death."

"I'm getting a lawyer." Koch picked up the phone, then put it down. "Get out of my office."

"With pleasure, Professor."

I had not said a word, but I was feeling wonderful. We had him. We left the office, retrieved my car, and I drove Jack to his station house.

"I think we can make trouble for him," Jack said. "As for prosecuting, that's up to the folks in Arizona. But if your friend the dean at Rimson wants to make Koch's life difficult, he can tell the administration at Columbia what you've dug up."

"I'll call him when I get home. And Marty McHugh. He's as guilty or innocent as Koch." I stopped for a light. "Do you really have those credit card receipts?"

"Would I lie?" He gave me a grin. "You don't have to take me the rest of the way. I'll walk. Nice to see you during the day." He leaned over and kissed me, opened the door, and strode down the street.

Someone honked behind me and I realized the light had turned green. I took off before I started an incident.

Dean Hershey was appropriately shocked. He promised to find all the students who had been brought to Rimson by Alfred Koch and further promised, if it turned out that they had been coerced into paying bribes, that he would notify his counterpart at Columbia. "He'll never be emeritus," he said, "with information like this."

Marty McHugh was enraged when I spoke to him. I told him that I had independent information that linked him, Millman, and Koch to the incident on the mountain and that the sheriff's office had his name and phone number.

After his ranting and raving, after absurd threats, I ended the conversation by hanging up and sitting back to clear my head. Then I called Andrew Franklin in Minnesota and apologized for doubting his claim that Heinz had taken off alone in a taxi to the airport. I was now convinced that Steve and Marty had indeed shared a cab. Even before he met Koch that evening, McHugh had planned something evil for Steve on the mountain the next day, and he wanted to keep his eye on him.

Finally, late in the day, I called Herb Fallon. He had returned from New York the evening before and listened carefully to what I told him.

"It's hard to believe," he said. "You think Marty and this guy Koch were planning to kill Steve?"

"I don't know, but I'd guess they just wanted to put

269

fear into him, get him to call off the lawsuit in the case of Koch, and suffer for Marty's being charged with plagiarism."

"So Heinz died and the others had twenty years of misery."

"It looks that way. I'm glad I got to know you, Herb."

"Same here. Maybe on our next trip we'll all go out to dinner. I'd like to meet your husband."

"We'll do it. Just let me know when you're making your next visit."

He promised he would.

29

It was a hot summer. From time to time I got reports on the investigation of Heinz Gruner's death and Alfred Koch's unseemly and unethical behavior. Dean Hershey was as good as his promise. He assured me that Koch, who was scheduled to retire soon, would not be named emeritus. It was a blow but a deserved one.

Meanwhile, Hershey had dug up many names of people who had paid bribes to Koch. Through his lawyer, Koch said he had decided to repay what he could. I wished Hilda had lived to hear about this, but I conveyed the information to Dr. Farley, who felt that justice was done. The amount that Koch would donate to the Heinz Gruner endowment was substantial and would buy many books. I considered this a blessing.

Late in the summer a small insured package arrived, addressed to me. It came from Hillside Village and I wondered what small piece of Hilda Gruner's life was inside.

The note was from Dr. Farley. He hoped I would wear and enjoy the two antique gold rings and the bracelet in three colors of gold that we had found in the bank box a few months earlier. I slipped a ring on and it fit perfectly. The other was almost as good a fit. One of them had a monogram that was hard to read, but definitely did have an H on it. The jewelry must have belonged to Hilda's mother or grandmother. I was glad Dr. Farley had not sold them for gold value. I would definitely enjoy wearing them. They would remind me of a family whose demise began on a mountain in Arizona because of the anger and misdeeds of three people who inadvertantly caused the death of the only innocent in the party.

The next day, I wrote my own check to the Rimson College Library.

Center Point Publishing

600 Brooks Road ● PO Box 1
Thorndike ME 04986-0001 USA

(207) 568-3717

US & Canada:
1 800 929-9108